"Such wonderful morsels! These astounding stories keep whirling around in my head."

Ann Menebroker, author of
Feast in Solitude and *Trying for the Ten Ring*

OTHER BOOKS BY
TODD WALTON

FICTION

Inside Moves

Forgotten Impulses

Louie & Women

Night Train

Ruby & Spear

Of Water and Melons

NONFICTION

Open Body: Creating Your Own Yoga

*The Writer's Path: A Guidebook
For Your Creative Journey*

BUDDHA
IN A
TEACUP

tales of enlightenment

TODD WALTON

LOST
COAST
PRESS

BUDDHA IN A TEACUP
tales of enlightenment
Copyright ©2008 by Todd Walton

Lost Coast Press
155 Cypress Street
Fort Bragg, California 95437
800-773-7782
Fax: 707-964-7531
http:\\www.cypresshouse.com
An audio version of this book is available from
underthetablebooks.com

Book production by Cypress House

Library of Congress Cataloging-in-Publication Data

Walton, Todd.
   Buddha in a teacup : tales of enlightenment / Todd Walton. --
1st ed.
     p. cm.
   ISBN 978-1-882897-95-7 (casebound : alk. paper)
   1. Buddhism--Fiction. 2. Buddhist stories, American.
   3. Spiritual life--Buddhism--Fiction. I. Title.
   PS3573.A474B83 2007
   813'.54--dc22   2007035317

Manufactured in the USA
2   4   6   8   9   7   5   3   1

For Marcia Sloane
and Kathleen Mooney

CONTENTS

AUTHOR'S NOTE

The reader will discover that tea plays a supporting role in many of these stories. This is in keeping with the history of Buddhism, which is profoundly entwined with the history of tea. I owe my little knowledge of tea to James Norwood Pratt.

Norwood's teaching technique, if one may call it that, is to prepare fine tea in my presence and, with the easy grace for which he is renowned, fill our cups. When we have tasted the tea, he listens to my assessment of the drink before telling me its name and where it comes from. He then elucidates why I find the tea earthy or sweet or grassy or reminiscent of chocolate. Thus, slowly, I have learned a bit about tea.

The stories contained in this volume spring from meditations on fundamental aspects of the dharma. I was inspired to such brevity by the *Palm of the Hand Stories* of Yasunari Kawabata.

I have scant interest in Buddhist dogma, but I am captivated by the wisdom and compassion of Buddha.

BUDDHA
IN A
TEACUP

*Little by little with patience and endurance
we must find the way for ourselves, find out
how to live with ourselves and with each other.*

Shunryu Suzuki

*Remember you are a Westerner. If you want to practice
an Eastern philosophy such as Tibetan Buddhism
you should take the essence and try to adapt it
to your cultural background and conditions.*

the thirteenth Dalai Lama

THE BEGGAR

Each morning on her way from the subway to her office in the pyramid building, Cheryl passes hundreds of beggars. And each evening on her way home, she passes most of the same beggars again. And there are beggars in the subway station, too.

Every few weeks, moved by a compulsion she has no explanation for, she empties the kitchen change jar into a paper bag and carries these hundreds of coins with her to work. On her way home at the end of the day, she gives this change to the only beggar she has ever admired. She has never told her husband or children what she does with the money, nor have they ever inquired about its repeated disappearance.

The man she gives this money to is tall and handsome, olive-skinned, with short brown hair and a well-trimmed beard. He is, she believes, close to her own age — forty-nine — and he wears the saffron robe of a Buddhist monk. He sits cross-legged on the sidewalk in front of the Costa Rican consulate, a stone's throw from the subway entrance. His back is perfectly straight, his head unbowed, and he sits absolutely still. He is not there in the mornings, but he is there every evening of Cheryl's workweek, except Wednesday evenings.

His large brass bowl sits on the ground directly in front of him. When money is dropped into the bowl he does not alter

his pose in the slightest, nor does he make any outward ges-
ture of thanks.

As the weeks and months and years go by, Cheryl finds herself thinking constantly about her favorite mendicant. He has
become something of a hero to her, though she knows nothing about him. She begins to wonder where he lives and what
he does with the money he collects. She has no idea when he
arrives at his begging post or when he leaves. She doesn't know
if he is mute or deaf. Does he beg on Saturdays and Sundays,
too? She only knows that he is there at six o'clock on Monday,
Tuesday, Thursday, and Friday evenings, sitting very still and
gazing straight ahead, receiving alms.

When she begins waking in the night from dreams in which
she and this man are fleeing together from some unseen terror,
she decides to change her path to work. She tells herself that if
she stops seeing him four times every week, she will eventually stop thinking about him. So she chooses another subway
stop, one a few blocks farther from the pyramid building, but
with only the rare beggar along her way.

   For the first week, her new route gives her sweet satisfac-
tion. She feels as if an enormous weight has been lifted from
her shoulders. She hadn't realized what a tremendous strain it
was for her to pass by all those poor people every day. And she
no longer sees *him* — that impeccably silent man in his golden
robe. She no longer sees his piercing eyes or his sensuous lips or

his beautifully formed hands resting palms up on his knees.

Still, she thinks of him constantly. She wakes exhausted from dreams of making love to him, of being his wife, his judge, his executioner. But it is only when she fails to sleep at all for three days and nights in succession, and feels herself dissolving into madness, that she decides to learn all she can about him.

She takes a week off from work, though she doesn't tell her husband she is doing so. On a cold morning in November, she rides the subway into the city at her usual hour. She stands on the sidewalk across the street from the Costa Rican consulate and waits for the object of her obsession to arrive.

At noon, his spot still vacant, Cheryl goes to a restaurant and fortifies herself with a meal, though she has little appetite. She has lost several pounds during the weeks of her growing concern about this man. Her husband believes she has finally discovered a successful diet.

Tired of standing, she is sitting on the sidewalk, her back against the wall of a bank, when he appears a block away — a golden flower in a river of darker flowers. He walks with stately grace, his begging bowl in his left hand, and a small rug, tightly rolled, in his right. When he has attained his place, he bows slightly in each of the four cardinal directions, places the bowl on the sidewalk, unfurls the rug, sits down upon it, and assumes his meditative posture, his eyes fixed on his bowl. He takes a deep breath and exhales, after which his breathing becomes imperceptible.

A moment passes, and now money begins to rain down, the bowl filling so quickly Cheryl is certain the monk will move to empty it, but he does not.

A man in a filthy black coat, a beggar Cheryl has seen a thousand times before, approaches the man in gold, nods to him, and empties the overflowing bowl into a small cardboard box.

A few minutes pass and the bowl is full once more. Now the veteran with one leg who sits in his wheelchair by the fire hydrant with a cat on his lap, rolls up to the man in gold, and leans down to dump the rich bowl into a red tartan sack.

And so it continues hour after hour until the last commuter has gone home and the bells of a distant church chime eight o'clock — seventy-seven beggars of every age and sex and color gifted by the begging bowl of the man in gold. Cheryl has tallied them in her notebook, the ink smeared by her tears.

A few minutes past eight, the man rises from his rug and stretches his arms to the sky. Now he bows to each of the four cardinal directions, rolls up his rug, picks up his empty bowl, and crosses the street to stand in front of Cheryl.

She looks up at him, speechless with love.

To which he replies softly, and with the force of a hurricane, "Hello, my dear friend."

Expectations

Karen is eager to have an interview with her teacher. She has been silent for seventeen days. She will be the last of the retreat participants to have a private hour with the renowned Buddhist. She is impatient to hear her thoughts given voice and to hear what he will say to her alone.

Her teacher is a small, round man from Tibet. Rumors abound that he is an alcoholic and a lecher, but nothing in her personal experience of him suggests he is anything but a wise and compassionate being.

"You," her friend Marie declared, "will be a great temptation to him. He is hopelessly attracted to beautiful young women."

Karen does not believe she will be sexually attractive to her teacher, nor does she aspire to be. Indeed, one of the gifts of her seventeen days of silent meditation is the pleasant absence of thoughts about her physical appearance.

She approaches her teacher's cottage at the appointed hour. The day has been warm, and now, as the sun hovers above the horizon, a cool breeze moves across the meadow of wild oats and tickles Karen's ears.

She knocks on the door — gray wood beginning to splinter. There is no response from within. She knocks again. No voice invites her to enter. Rather than turn away, she pushes lightly on the door and it swings open.

The small room holds two armchairs facing a black wood-stove. A large, spotlessly clean window gives a view to the west of brown hills descending to the sea. Beneath this window is a small bed, the mattress covered with a yellow sheet. Karen's teacher and a young woman are asleep in each other's arms. They are naked, the young woman's curly black hair glistening with sweat.

"What did I expect?" Karen asks, watching her teacher's face.

She wants him to open his eyes and reply to her. But even when a shiny blue fly lands in his nostril, her teacher does not stir.

Mama

"Can you tell me," asks Sweeney, handing the teapot to McDougall, "what this is worth?"

McDougall, a portly man with a gray handlebar mustache, takes the little pearly white teapot in his big fleshy hands and nods slowly. "Baleek," he says quietly. "Irish porcelain. Late eighteen hundreds. Extremely rare. I'll have to examine her with a magnifying glass, but if this is the original glaze, and she's flawless, I'd say she's worth ten thousand dollars. Possibly more. And I'll tell you right now, I want her."

Sweeney, a slender man with brown hair turning gray, had hoped to get thirty or forty dollars for the old thing. Desperate for money, he had finally done what he'd been avoiding for three years. He'd gone through the two boxes of stuff left to him by his mother. In the first of the boxes he found only memorabilia — pictures and letters. But the second box contained the teapot, six matching cups and saucers, and a matching sugar bowl and creamer.

"That much?" he says, trying not to show too much astonishment at McDougall's estimate of the teapot's worth. "And what if I had the matching cups and saucers and things?"

McDougall gazes thoughtfully at Sweeney, his right eyebrow rising dramatically. "*Six* cups and saucers?"

"Yes," says Sweeney, holding his breath. "And a sugar bowl and creamer."

McDougall carefully sets the teapot down on the table between them. "A complete set of this Baleek, circa 1870, in excellent condition, would be worth at least fifty thousand dollars, and possibly a great deal more."

"Why so much?" asks Sweeney, staggered by the sum.

"Well, first of all we're talking about extremely rare and fragile ceramics that are nearly a hundred and fifty years old. A complete, original set outside of a museum is virtually unheard of in this day and age." He pauses. "Handles intact?"

"Yes," says Sweeney, turning to go. "I'll be back with them in twenty minutes."

"No, no, no!" cries McDougall, emphatically shaking his head. "I will bring my padded carrying case and come with you."

"Excuse the mess," says Sweeney, unlocking the door to his apartment.

"I'm used to messes," says McDougall, following Sweeney into the cramped little room. "In the mud lie the nuggets."

The place smells sour, the sink full of dirty dishes, clothes strewn about the floor, the squalid bed unmade. On a rickety table by the only window, six cups on six saucers surround a sugar bowl and creamer, each piece the same pearly white as the teapot. McDougall reverently approaches this still life, his eyes wide with wonder. When he is satisfied that the pieces are immaculate, he turns to Sweeney and says, "I will be happy to write you a check for fifty thousand dollars."

"And I will be happy to accept it," says Sweeney, his tired eyes filling with tears.

When the rare and delicate tea set is safely packed away, the padded case closed and locked, McDougall says, "Now, if you don't mind, could you tell me what you know about the set and where your mother got it?"

"I don't know anything about it except that my mother's mother was British, so maybe it was hers."

"You don't remember your mother using it?"

"No," says Sweeney, his voice full of disdain, "but then I don't remember much of anything about her."

"When did she die?"

"Three years ago."

"You were her only heir?"

He nods. "She didn't leave me anything except a box of photographs and the tea things."

"Would it be a terrible imposition if I looked through those photographs?"

"No, not at all." Sweeney hands him a well-worn cardboard box. "In fact, you can have them if you want."

McDougall takes the box from him. "Have you looked at these?"

"No," says Sweeney, shaking his head. "My mother hated me. She used to call me her big mistake. These wouldn't mean anything to me. And now, if you'll excuse me, I want to get to the bank before it closes."

With the Baleek safely installed in his vault, McDougall makes a strong pot of black tea and sits down to examine the photographic legacy of Sweeney's mother. There are hundreds of photos, and on the back of each is a note to Sweeney. The largest picture is of Sweeney as a boy of seven or eight having a tea party with his mother. They are using the Baleek set. On the back of the photograph Sweeney's mother has written

Here we are acting out the Mad Hatter's tea party from Alice in Wonderland. That's my mother's old Baleek tea set, which she got from her mother who got it as a wedding gift in 1872. Amazing none of the pieces ever broke. You even had tea parties with your friends Raymond and Cecily, but nothing ever broke. Proof of angels, if you ask me.

You know, Dearie, I wish I could have left you buckets of money, but all I have is this tea set. I hope it brings you joy.
        Mama

Retreat

The five-day retreat begins with a walking meditation, during which Andrew obsesses about everything he has left behind. At lunch, he eats three huge helpings of rice and vegetables, but during the afternoon sitting session he cannot remember eating anything. He burps, and the flavors of chard and vinegar tickle his taste buds. For a fleeting moment he sees again his brimming bowl of food. All his other thoughts have been about his stock portfolio, the car he wants to buy, his failing relationship with Stella, and his strategy for gaining an investment advantage in a promising new technology.

After supper, he attends the dharma talk given by a Buddhist nun. Her opening words are, "Why do we fear this moment? *This* moment. Here. Right now." That is all Andrew hears. For the rest of the talk, he is consumed by scenarios of the stock market going way up or way down. As he imagines the market rising, he becomes so excited he can barely stay seated. As he imagines the market falling, his limbs grow heavy and cold.

Walking to the dormitory following the talk — the road awash in moonlight — Andrew hears someone ask, "What did you think of her?" For a long moment, he cannot separate the voice and the question from his thoughts about what clothes he should wear to the meeting with the men who own the new technology he wants to invest in. With a tremendous effort, he brings his attention to the present moment and finds he is quite alone.

On the road ahead of him, several people are standing together looking up at two white owls perched in an enormous oak tree. As the owls launch themselves into the night sky, Andrew returns to his dilemma of what to wear to his meeting with the new technologists.

He barely sleeps a wink that night, imagining himself attending dozens of meetings, changing clothes countless times, making and losing several fortunes. He finally falls asleep a few minutes before a monk enters the dormitory and strikes a gong to summon the retreat participants to early morning meditation.

Moments after sitting down in the zendo, Andrew falls asleep and tumbles off his cushion, bumping into the woman next to him. Deeply chagrined, he sits in abject misery for the rest of the hour-long session, his body aching from head to toe as he rehearses his apology. When the gong sounds, he can barely rouse himself to rise.

On his way to breakfast, feeling utterly drained and defeated, Andrew comes to the conclusion that this retreat is a colossal waste of his valuable time. He gobbles a bowl of hot cereal and hurries out of the cafeteria determined to withdraw. He skips down the gravel path to the office, elated to be leaving.

"What a gorgeous place," he says, smiling up at the billowy white clouds scudding through the brilliant blue sky. A breeze engulfs him in the scent of jasmine blossoms, and he slows to marvel at a bevy of delicate yellow butterflies fluttering drunkenly around a stand of voluptuous red lilies.

He steps through the open door of the cottage where the office is housed and finds a man speaking to the nun who gave the previous evening's dharma talk. The man is saying, "...just doesn't feel right...couldn't get my head into the right space...need to talk to my wife...think I might have bounced a check...maybe next time."

The man gives Andrew a sheepish grin and scurries out the door. Andrew gazes at the nun — a short, stout woman with a freshly shaved head. She finishes writing something in a large ledger and turns her gaze upon him. Her eyes are green and deeply set. There is something impish about her face — playful and mysterious. She smiles and says, "Hello."

"Hello," he replies, surprised and yet not surprised to hear himself say, "I want to thank you for your talk last night. I was barely here. I'm only just now arriving."

She wrinkles her nose and whispers, "Me, too."

MEAT

He had planned everything so carefully, Marvin had. And now, what with a long delay due to unforeseen road construction, a flat tire despite brand new steel-belted radials, and a state agricultural inspector at the Nevada border who found Dipa's turban possibly indicative of forbidden foodstuffs, they are hours late for, and ninety-five miles away from, their rendezvous with Mary, Marvin's wife, at the only vegetarian restaurant for hundreds of miles around.

Dipa, a tiny, bird-like man with brown skin, his dress a loose gown of gray cotton, is not the least disturbed by the various delays in their journey. He turns to Marvin and says, "Perhaps this next village will provide us with some tasty comestibles. I haven't eaten since I left Bombay two days ago."

"I am *so* sorry," says Marvin, grimacing sympathetically. "Two days? You must be faint from hunger."

"I believe I am." Dipa giggles. "Low blood sugar."

Marvin — a heavy-limbed man with wispy gray hair, the reluctant chauffeur of his wife's guru — terminates cruise control and slows his enormous silver Mercedes to a crawl as they enter Shotgun, population 97, home to Lacey's General Store and two taverns: the Buckshot and the 12-Gauge.

"There." Dipa points at the brilliant neon sign above the Buckshot — a blinking fountain of blue and green and red light erupting from the muzzle of a gigantic magenta shotgun. "Surely they will have food."

"The thing is," says Marvin, breaking into one of his exceedingly odiferous sweats, "that's a rough and tumble kinda place. Mostly cowboys. I don't think…"

"Well, then that one," says the holy man, pointing at the 12-Gauge, its neon sign also featuring a colossal shotgun, turquoise, breaking open to receive two glowing orange cartridges from an unseen source, the gun snapping shut as gold and red fire erupts from its double barrels.

"It's the same sort of place," says Marvin, shaking his head emphatically. "I'm not sure they'll have anything but beer and peanuts."

"Two fine foodstuffs," says Dipa, nodding enthusiastically.

Marvin parks amidst a herd of enormous pickup trucks in front of the 12-Gauge. "I'll just dart in and grab us a snack," he says, frowning at the gravity of his mission. "Probably be better if you waited here."

"I must pee," says Dipa, opening his door and leaping out. "And I'm very hungry."

"But these are violent rednecks!" cries Marvin, panicking. "They'll…who knows what they'll do when they see your turban and your…dress."

"I believe otherwise," says Dipa, skipping to the double doors and pushing them open before Marvin can finish punching in the twelve-digit anti-theft combination on his remote auto manager pocket computer.

"Jesus," Marvin murmurs, whipping out his mobile phone and calling Mary.

She answers on the first ring. "Marvin?"

"We're in Shotgun," he says breathlessly. "He just went into the 12-Gauge. I'm going in after him."

"What are you talking about?"

"Just so you know," he whispers, putting a shoulder to the saloon door. "Shotgun. 12-Gauge."

Dipa is nowhere to be seen. Four men, none of them wearing cowboy hats, are sitting at the bar tended by an elderly woman wearing bifocals, her long gray hair in braids. A middle-aged man is playing pool with his nine-year-old granddaughter. A football game watched by no one is showing on a big-screen television, the sound off, while the jukebox plays an old Johnny Mathis recording of *Moon River* — the big room redolent with the scent of grilled steak.

"Excuse me," says Marvin, addressing the woman behind the bar, "do you serve anything vegetarian?"

"Potatoes." She nods pleasantly. "And we can make you a salad and fry you up some veggies. The menu's all steak, but we can make you just about anything you want."

"Oh, it's not for me." He grins anxiously at the men without cowboy hats. "It's for my friend from India. The man with the turban? He observes extremely strict dietary limitations."

"I would love a beer," says Dipa, mounting the barstool beside Marvin and bowing graciously to the bartender. "Please allow me to buy the next round of drinks for these good gentlemen."

Marvin's mobile phone vibrates violently in his pocket, clattering against his miniature computer. "Excuse me," he says, hurrying to the men's room. "I'll be right back."

In the bathroom, the walls covered with old record jackets from the early days of folk rock — Quicksilver Messenger Service, Buffalo Springfield, Big Brother and the Holding Company — Marvin presses the phone to his cheek and says to Mary, "It's okay. I've got things under control. We'll grab a quick bite and be on our way. He was famished. I don't think we'll have any trouble. Thank God it's not a Friday night."

An hour and several beers later, Bea, the bartender, waitress, hostess, chef, and owner of the 12-Gauge, serves Marvin his T-bone steak, rare, with baked potato and green beans, and for the holy man she has prepared a generous helping of curried vegetables and potatoes with yogurt and red-hot salsa on the side.

"Many thanks," says Dipa, bowing to her. "Just like home."

Marvin is about to cut into his singed slab of cow flesh when it occurs to him that the sight of the bloody meat might be offensive to Dipa. He forces a smile. "Does this bother you? My eating meat?"

"No," says Dipa, contemplating his food before eating.

"But *you* would never eat meat," says Marvin, sneering at his steak and feeling mean and unevolved.

"I have eaten meat," says Dipa, nodding. "And I would have eaten meat tonight if there had been no other choice."

"But it's a sin, isn't it?" Marvin stabs at his steak and winces. "Do you call them sins? Or taboos?"

"There is a story about Buddha coming to a village at dusk," says Dipa, smiling warmly at Marvin. "No one there recognizes him as anything other than a simple monk. He is given shelter for the night by a humble woman who lives in a small hut. For Buddha's meal, she serves him a bowl of stew she has been cooking for several hours. There is goat meat in this stew, but Buddha understands that no intention on his part caused the death of the goat, so he eats in gratitude for those beings who have lived and died so that he might go on living, and in gratitude to the woman who has shown him such generosity." Dipa winks at Marvin. "That's all I teach. Intention and gratitude and generosity."

ONE FORTUNATE ATTACHMENT

Had they been lovers, had they tried to live together, or had either of them ever mentioned the surreal disparities in their financial situations, she doubts they could have shared even a moment of what has become the spiritual and emotional foundation of her life — a weekly meeting at his tiny flat where they share tea, poetry, meditation, and loving admiration.

He is a poet of local repute, a handsome, gregarious man of fifty-three, his flat little more than monk's quarters, his wardrobe minimalist, his personal habits rigorously healthy since the end of his lengthy addiction to alcohol. He lives rent free in exchange for maintaining his and five other units in an older two-story apartment building in North Beach. Money for groceries and tea comes to him as a consequence of the unlicensed psychotherapy and spiritual counseling he provides to a wide range of acquaintances. His fees for services are determined by the whims of his clients, many of who are as unmonied as he.

Much of his ample free time is spent in walking, writing, and reading. He meditates without fail for an hour in the morning and for an hour at dusk. His name is Theodore, and not a one of his hundreds of friends calls him Ted.

Her name is Elise. She is forty-nine, though at first glance this seems wholly implausible. She moves with the energy of a dancer in her twenties and is possessed of archetypal beauty — slender and shapely — her features a deft blend of English and Spanish lines of grace. Until her marriage at thirty-eight, she was a well-known fashion model.

She lives in a mansion in Pacific Heights, a palatial home maintained through the hard work of a household staff of five: a gardener, a live-in chef, a housekeeper, the housekeeper's assistant, and a personal secretary named Charles, who also frequently serves as Elise's driver.

She maintains a busy social schedule, serves prominently on the boards of several charities, practices yoga with her personal yoga teacher *every* day (Charles and the chef often practice with her), and she is a member of the most exclusive health spa in the city where she avails herself of frequent massages, beauty treatments, and saunas.

Elise's husband, Daniel, twenty years her senior, is frequently abroad on business. At the beginning of their marriage, Elise often traveled with him, but she no longer will. She has yet to admit to anyone — including herself — that she stays year-round in San Francisco because she cannot bear to miss her three hours a week with Theodore.

Daniel knows of his wife's connection to the poet, and he has no misgivings about it — his own relationship with Elise being straightforward and passionless. She is his charming and beautiful companion when he requires such for publicity and social propriety. She maintains his principal residence with a pleasing flair for beauty and serenity. She gives him no trouble, keeps him in the public eye as befits a man of his wealth and power, and completes the picture he has of what it is to be an eminently successful man.

He trusts Elise completely, though this trust has nothing to do with sexual loyalty, something he long ago abandoned as impractical. No, what Daniel trusts is that Elise will never do anything to harm or inconvenience him. He trusts that *his* need of her will always supersede anyone else's need of her — that her life will, in essence, be built around him.

Elise stops to buy flowers at a Chinese market a block from Theodore's apartment. Lil, the elderly matriarch of the store, shuffles out from behind the counter and takes the white roses as Elise selects them from the big black bucket of blooms.

"Seven," says Elise, smiling at Lil. "Today is our seventh anniversary."

"Not so long marry," says Lil, clipping the ends of the stems. "I marry sixty-one year."

"Oh, not marriage," says Elise, blushing brightly. "Seven years of knowing Theodore."

Lil nods as she wraps the flowers in newspaper. "Any else today?"

Elise doesn't hear her. She has been struck deaf by the irrevocable truth of her desire to become Theodore's mate.

"Fruit, maybe," says Lil, tapping a big yellow mango. "Sweet."

There is a note pinned to Theodore's door.

> *Elise,*
> *I will be home shortly. Minor emergency.*
> *Please let yourself in and put the kettle on.*
>   *Theo*

"Home," she says, slipping her key into his lock. "I'm home."

As the water falls from the faucet into the kettle, Elise relaxes into the sensation of spaciousness she always feels in Theodore's diminutive flat. She sets the kettle on the flame and turns to look out the window that forms the top half of the back door. The distant bay is dotted with sailboats, the sky full of menacing gray clouds.

She loses herself in visions of a deluge so strong and lasting that she cannot leave. She sees herself undressing with Theodore by candlelight, sharing his bed, and making love with him throughout the long, stormy night. "In the morning," she says aloud, "we'll run away together and start over in a place where no one knows us."

She has rarely been alone in Theodore's home. He is almost always there when she arrives — the water ready for tea. Only twice before in seven years has she waited for him, and never for more than a few moments.

She is drawn to Theodore's writing table where a letter sits in the center of the otherwise empty surface. Written in a neat hand on pale gray stationery, it says:

Dear Theo,

It is with enormous pleasure that I, acting as representative of the unanimous board of directors, invite you to make your principle home for the rest of your life at Quail Valley zendo. The cottage on the rim of Coyote Gulch is being renovated in anticipation of your arrival. As we discussed on the phone, money for food, clothing, and supplies, such as you demand, will be available to you from the general fund. Travel expenses will also…

Elise snatches the letter and crushes it violently in her hands. She turns away from the desk and stumbles to the big brown armchair where she always sits during her visits with Theodore. Overcome with dizziness and heat, she pulls off her coat and flings it aside, growling, "I hate you, Daniel."

Her feet begin to throb and burn. She unlaces her boots and yanks them off, hurling them down at the rug where Theodore usually sits during their visits.

Suffocating, she stands up and pulls off her sweater and blouse, unbuckles her belt, and steps out of her slacks. The kettle begins to scream. She crosses to the stove wearing only her white silk underwear — her body on fire.

Theodore opens his door to Elise, naked, twirling around and around in the center of his room.

He smiles in wonder and says, "I'm not going. I'm not ready to leave you."

She comes to a graceful halt, her body glistening with sweat, her eyes bright and clear.

"I want you to go," she says with utter calm. "In time, I will follow."

Ten Thousand Things

Esme watches herself in the mirror putting on lipstick. She frowns at her myriad wrinkles, and snorts at the absurdity of the thought that she has grown old. She is eighty-six.

Esme is standing in front of her house when her son, Bill, arrives. He is fifty-eight. Before he can get out of his big blue pickup truck, Esme barks at him. "Move the garbage can out to the curb. Sweep up these pine needles. They're unsightly."

"Ma," he says, working hard to stay calm. "How about saying hello?"

She flounces around the nose of his truck to the passenger door as if nothing has been said by either of them. She climbs in and puts on her seatbelt. "I don't know why I bother," she complains bitterly. "They haven't had a decent fair in twenty years."

"We don't have to go," he says, gripping the steering wheel. "This is supposed to be for fun, Ma."

"Of course we have to go," she says, sneering imperiously. "It's a tradition."

Inching toward the fairgrounds, traffic snarled, Esme shakes her head and says, "I told you so."

Bill turns to her. "Ma. How old am I?"

"Horrendous heat," she says, fanning herself and making a spluttering sound. The day is mild, the truck air-conditioned. "Why do they always have the fair when the weather is so awful?" She sighs. "Worse now, of course. *We* never had smog like this."

Bill resists the temptation to point out that she is part of the current We. He closes his eyes, wondering again why he bothers to do anything for his mother.

They come to a dead stop. Esme sighs — an audible moan — exactly as she has sighed ten thousand times before, but this time, this ten thousandth time, something gives way inside of Bill, something in his heart. He touches his sternum with the middle three fingers of his right hand and for one stunning moment he feels such overwhelming pain that his vision abandons him in a flash of light — and the pain is gone.

He turns to look at his mother. She is glaring at the road ahead as she always does, but there is something about her face he has not been aware of before — nobility and strength.

"What could it possibly *be*?" she asks, her voice no longer grating but musical — a viola taken to the edge of sharpness. "We aren't going *any*where."

"It's the Grand Coulee Dam, Ma," he says, feeling a gush of love for her. "They brought it in last night with sixty-five thousand blimps."

"Don't be absurd!" she cries, trying to contain her mirth, but the word **blimps** unglues her and she bursts into laughter.

In line to buy tickets, Esme scowls at the list of admission prices. "This is an outrage," she hisses. "This is robbery. Why…when I was a girl it was practically free."

"Free love," says Bill, stepping up to the ticket window and beaming at the sweaty young woman glued to her stool. "One outraged old woman and her suddenly euphoric son."

"She your mom?" asks the young woman — two tickets emerging from two slots in the metal counter.

"From her womb I came," says Bill, feeling downright reverent.

"Then she's in free. It's moms in free this afternoon."

"You here that, Ma? Free."

"Don't believe it," says Esme, her eyes narrowing. "They're just trying to sell us something."

In the beer garden, Bill sipping stout, Esme having lemonade, three knobby-kneed men in faded lederhosen play a peppy little polka.

"Shall we dance, Ma?" asks Bill, nodding. "I think we shall."

"Don't be absurd," she says, frowning at him. "With my hip? Are you drunk?"

"I've had a conversion," he says, seeing everything as if for the first time. "I stepped over a line or my heart broke or I forgave you or I forgave myself. I don't know. But I'm not mad at you anymore. I actually love you."

She shrugs. "Well, la dee da."

"Shoe bop shoe wah," he says, bouncing his eyebrows.

She looks at her watch. "It's late. We haven't seen the quilts yet."

Making their way through a flood of humanity, they are momentarily separated — Esme crying, "Bill! Don't leave me!"

Bill makes his way to her and says, "Here I am, Ma."

She clutches his arm and stamps her feet. "This is awful. I hate this. They ruined everything. It used to be so nice and now look at it. Garbage everywhere. No place to sit. The restrooms are filthy."

"Do you want to leave or do you want to see the quilts?"

"I *want* to see the quilts," she groans. "But how will we ever get there?"

"We will sing songs," he says, taking her hand. "From all our favorite musicals."

"Don't be ridiculous," she says, allowing him to lead her along.

"We're *off* to see the wizard," he begins. "The wonderful wizard of Oz."

"Judy Garland was a drug addict," says Esme, nodding emphatically. "I could never forgive her for that."

"Why not?" says Bill, giving his mother's hand a gentle squeeze. "Let's forgive her."

"Oh, look," says Esme, pointing at the sign above the pavilion. "We're here."

"I never gave a hoot about quilts," says Bill, sitting beside his mother on a cushioned bench to take a long look at the grand prizewinner. "Now I'm in love."

"These are nothing," says Esme, dismissing everything in the vast room with a wave of her hand. "When I was a girl, we *really* knew how to make quilts."

"This is phantasmagoric," says Bill, gesturing at the giant blue field dotted with stars and sheep and bubbles and clouds. "I *believe* in this."

"It's big," says Esme, nodding. "I'll give it that."

"You're just you," he says, looking at her. "And I'm just me."

"I'm out of gas," she says, leaning against him. "Take me home?"

He walks her to her front door. "Shall I come in? Cook you dinner? Rub your feet?"

She turns away and fits her key into the lock. "Not like it used to be," she sighs, opening the door. "Don't come in. Place is a mess."

"Ma?" he says, deftly sending the word into her heart.

"Yes, dear," she says, turning to gaze at him. "That's me."

WISHING

Everything is better than Nathan hoped it would be. The little island with its one elegant hotel is even more paradisiacal than he'd dreamed. Nearly all the tourists have returned to the mainland, and the food in the hotel restaurant is exquisite, the wine surprisingly good. And the beach is the beach of Nathan's fantasies — fine white sand sloping gently to a turquoise lagoon with a backdrop of palm trees beneath a cerulean sky.

Nathan hopes to meet a beautiful woman on this beach. She will have a lovely body and a gorgeous smile. She will be ripe to meet the love of her life, and Nathan will be that love.

Nathan is forty-seven. The woman he hopes to meet will be in her thirties. In his fantasy, the woman reveals her formidable charm and sophistication in the very first words she speaks to him. She finds his wry sense of humor irresistible, and when she learns that he owns a successful company and a fine home in San Francisco, she confesses to a lifelong desire to live in California.

The beach is empty. There is not a breath of wind. Nathan imagines walking to the end of the white sand — a half mile away — and encountering the woman on his way back. The top of his head, which is bald, begins to ache from too much sun, so he puts on his new straw hat, though it doesn't fit him well and makes him sweat profusely. He ordered the hat from a catalogue of Australian outback gear. The models in the catalogue are muscular, ruggedly handsome men wearing their hats tipped at rakish angles. Nathan tips his hat at an angle, too, though he is not muscular or ruggedly handsome. His jungle camouflage shorts and beige sun shirt came from this same catalogue of outback attire.

A dozen yards from the hotel, the soles of Nathan's tender feet begin to burn on the sand, so he hurries to the water's edge where tiny waves lap the shore. Standing in the deliciously cool water, Nathan is consumed by visions of the woman he hopes to meet. He imagines swimming in the lagoon with her, watching the sunset with her from the hotel verandah as they sip icy rum drinks, and going to his suite to make love with her.

The day is far hotter than Nathan expected it would be. Halfway down the beach, he is exhausted and thirsty. Finding himself entirely alone, he strips down to his bright red underwear and dives into the blissfully cool water.

"Oh, God, yes," he croons, rolling onto his back and letting out a huge sigh of relief.

Thousands of tiny silver fish dart through the water around him, flashing in the sunlight like diamonds. Two white terns drift above him in the depthless sky. The rhythmic whispering of the surf lulls him into peacefulness he has not known since childhood. And into this peace comes a memory of being a boy sitting on a high stool in a warm kitchen, his beloved grandmother kneading dough, her cheeks rosy from the oven's heat, a plate of freshly baked cookies steaming in the winter sunlight.

Now a feathery white cloud appears in the sky above him and he trembles to realize that he is no longer a little boy, but a man floating on his back in the waters of the Caribbean, a man with no idea of how long he has been drifting there. With some reluctance, he allows his legs to sink, and he becomes upright in the water. He looks back at the beach where his clothes should be, but to his horror they have disappeared.

Panic-stricken, he swims to shore. Seeing no footprints other than his own on the wet sand, he assumes that a thief or thieves must have emerged from the palm trees, crossed the short expanse of sand, and taken his clothes and his wallet full of credit cards.

He stands on the beach, frozen in fear, imagining the thieves boarding a jet and flying to San Francisco. Knowing his address from his driver's license, they park a large van in front of his house and steal all his valuable possessions.

He runs toward the hotel, seeing himself canceling his credit cards and warning the police in San Francisco that robbers may very well be on their way to ransack his home.

"Fortunately," he gasps, "I left my travelers checks in my room, so..." But wait! His room keys were in his shorts. He sees the thieves — two shadowy figures — finding the traveler's checks in his suitcase and taking his portable computer.

Now a woman appears in the distance. She is walking toward him on the wet sand at the water's edge. She moves with languid ease, her body slender and shapely, her long reddish brown hair caught in a ponytail. Her straw hat is the twin of the one

Nathan just lost — all but two of the buttons on her long-sleeved white shirt undone over her bright pink bikini.

Nathan's entire being becomes focused on his stomach bulging over his bright red underwear. Terrified of meeting this woman so undressed, he plunges back into the water and swims away until he is farther out than he has ever been in his life. Yet as he turns to look back at the shore, he sees the woman swimming out to him, coursing through the water like some fantastic mermaid.

In no time she is treading water beside him, flashing a brilliant smile.

"Hello," she says, her voice enchanting. "I was hoping I could entice you to swim with me. We seem to be the only ones here and they say it's not safe to swim alone."

"Oh," he says, dazzled by her sparkling eyes, "I thought you were coming to rescue me."

She laughs. "Maybe I am. My name is Stephanie Anders. Who are you?"

"Nathan," he replies, his heart pounding. "Nathan Porter."

"Nathan," she says thoughtfully. "I've always loved that name. Where are you from?"

"San Francisco. And you?"

"I was born in San Francisco," she says, her voice deepening mysteriously. "But I've been living in Spain for the last few years. In Barcelona. I'm writing a book about the new generation of Spanish artists."

"I've always wanted to go to Spain," he says wistfully. "But for some reason I never have. Gone."

"You'd love it," she says, swimming closer, "though I must admit I prefer France. I love the language so."

"It is a beautiful language," says Nathan, overcome by a fierce wave of anxiety. "I've got to go in now. Sorry. I...I was just robbed. I've got to cancel my credit cards and call the police. Sorry."

"Robbed?" she says, frowning incredulously. "Here? I've never heard of anyone being..."

"Yes," he says, swimming toward shore. "They must have been hiding in the jungle waiting for me to go in the water."

"Are you sure?" she asks, swimming beside him. "I've been coming here for years and..."

"Of *course* I'm sure," he snarls, wishing she would disappear — hating that she will see him in his too tight red underwear in the glaring sun, his stomach bulging. "You think I'm an idiot?"

"No," she says, slowing down to let him go ahead. "I was only trying to help."

That evening on the hotel veranda, the sky aflame with golden clouds, Nathan waits for Stephanie to appear. He is eager to tell her the good news about his things — that they were found exactly where he left them.

"Sometimes people get disoriented when they first go into the lagoon," explained the hotel manager. "Something about the light, the white sand, the sameness of the palms. Happens all the time. But we've never had anything stolen here."

Nathan imagines Stephanie standing at the entrance to the dining room, a diaphanous dress clinging to her lovely form. He sees himself rising gallantly and crossing the room to her. He hears himself saying, "Please forgive me for my unreasonable outburst. I was disoriented and upset. I hope you'll let me make it up to you."

The golden clouds turn gray — dusk laying claim to the island. A waiter moves silently about the veranda, lighting candles. Nathan finishes his third glass of wine and beckons to the hotel manager, a dapper man with gray hair and a handlebar mustache.

"Tell me," says Nathan, finding it difficult to focus. "You have a guest here named Stephanie Anders. I'm wondering…"

"Oh, yes," says the manager, nodding slowly. "She left this afternoon. A sudden change of plans."

CHANGE

What was her name? She modeled for him twice. The four paintings he made of her sold before the paint was dry. Something about her angularity — a hunger in her bones. Or was it the sorrow in her eyes — the first glimmering of old age?

A gigantic face looms before him, startling him. "Hello, Boo Boo," says a voice coming from enormous lips on their way to press a kiss against his cheek. "You poopy? Need a change?"

Huge hands close around his middle, lifting him from the cushioned chair. He moans softly, a sound his mother hears as the beginning of language.

I'm Walter Casey, he tries to say. *The artist.*

But only the most primitive sounds escape him, his brand new larynx yet untrained.

Helpless on the changing table, his mother frees him from his itchy pajamas and lifts away his soiled diapers. He sighs with relief to have his bum free in the open air. She wipes him clean, cooing as she pulls the string on the musical bear — *Twinkle, Twinkle, Little Star* playing for the thousandth time.

Mendelssohn he tries to say. *Mozart. Anything but this ice-cream-truck twaddle.*

She sits with him in dappled shade, chuckling at how ravenously he feeds on her.

Maria. That was her name. She wanted to make love with me. All I had to do was ask. But I was too arrogant. No. Afraid.

His mother pulls him off her nipple. He begins to shriek in despair.

"Hold on, Boo Boo. Switching breasts, that's all."

He falls asleep and drifts through layers of time to

a snarling dog lunging at him
his father saying You Are No Son of Mine
forms appearing on his canvas as if by magic
mother clutching his hand as death takes her
his lover kissing his throat

The man who comes to visit every day is not the baby's father. The baby's father is bearded and stays in the house throughout the night. This other man has no beard. He only stays for an hour or so, speaking out loud to the baby, but conversing silently with Walter Casey.

How are you feeling? asks the man.

I forget more than I remember now.

Yes, says the man. *Soon you will forget almost everything that came before this life.*

But I don't want to forget.

What do you wish to remember?

Everything.
Choose one thing.
The baby laughs. The man laughs, too.

The creek tumbles down through the wooded gorge — a sensual chill in the air. Yellow leaves drift through slanting rays of sunlight and settle on the forest floor. Walter stands at the water's edge, the tip of his fishing rod pointing toward the sun, his line disappearing into a deep pool. Tomorrow is his seventeenth birthday.

His mother appears on the ridge above him. She is small in the distance, lovely and strong. She waves to let him know it is time to come home for supper. Walter waves back to her and reels in his line. Now he looks up at the falling leaves, at the branches of the aspens, at the billowy white clouds in the gray blue sky, and he begins to weep.

"Don't cry, Boo Boo," says his father, lifting him from his crib. "Here we are. Don't be afraid."

I am not afraid. I was remembering the happiest moment of my other life.

"Don't cry, Boo Boo," says the gentle, bearded man. "Mama will feed you. Everything is okay."

Beginning Practice

Joseph, a self-conscious young man with a shaved head, sits at a small table in the darkest corner of the café, writing a poem. The first two lines came easily to him.

broken glass, green and brown —
a necklace round the tree trunk

Beyond that, he has drawn a blank. He wants to say something poignant and meaningful about the trees that grow up through the sidewalks of the concrete city, but every new line he writes sounds trite.

He puts down his pen, rubs his eyes, and decides to have a cup of tea. He prefers coffee to tea, but the three people he admires most — his mentor at the Zen center, his yoga instructor, his favorite poet — all drink tea, so he is trying to develop the habit. His father, from whom he is estranged, drinks quarts of coffee every day.

Stepping to the counter, Joseph smiles at the word **BUDDHA** printed in large block letters across the pale blue T-shirt worn by Irene, the young woman who works the morning shift at Café Muse. Irene is a voluptuous brunette, each of her carefully plucked eyebrows pierced with seven gold rings, her dark brown eyes enormous. The *U* in Buddha rides atop her right breast, the *H* atop her left.

"Green tea, please," says Joseph, raising his eyes from Irene's breasts to her eyes. "Are you a Buddhist?"

"Sort of," she says with a shrug. "Are you?"

"Absolutely," he replies, his chest swelling with pride. "I've been going to the Zen center for years."

This is not precisely true. Joseph has been going twice a week for three months.

"Is that, like, free?" asks Irene as she prepares his tea. "Can you just…go in?"

"We have regular meditation times." Joseph's voice deepens with authority. "I generally go in the evenings. Seven to nine."

She hands him a white mug and a small black teapot. "I'll check it out. That's two dollars."

"Cool," says Joseph, eager to prolong the conversation. "So where did you get your T-shirt?"

"They're my favorite band," she says, turning around to show him the back. The word *GROOVES* is written in crimson italics. Irene turns back around and peers down at her breasts. "Buddha Grooves. They're kind of world-beat reggae with some metal and hip-hop. Very danceable."

"Are *they* Buddhists?" asks Joseph, his tone disdainful.

"Is that like a big deal?" she asks, frowning at him. "Knowing if someone is a Buddhist or not? I thought Buddha loved everybody no matter what. Wasn't that why he stuck around instead of going off to nirvana? So he could spread the light?" She looks deep into Joseph's eyes. "Isn't Buddhism about becoming more and more open to what actually *is*, instead of just following some old dogma?"

Hearing these words from her, the blockade between his mind and his heart — an amalgam of fear and sorrow — begins to crumble.

GENEROSITY

Tess, a slender woman with brilliant blue eyes and long gray hair, lives in Golden Gate Park — her camping place known only to her.

"I don't leave anything there when I come out. If you were standing right on it, you wouldn't know anyone lived there because it's just a place along the way. I leave no indentation. Even if you found me there you wouldn't know I lived there because I might just be a tourist sitting in the park. I only have my knapsack." She smiles. "The only way they could bust me is if they found me there at night, but no one comes there at night. Except me. It's such an unlikely place for a person to live."

Tess and a middle-aged man named Thomas are having lunch at a café a few blocks from the park. Thomas has known Tess for three years. They met at an arts faire in downtown San Francisco where Tess was selling handmade greeting cards. Each card contains one of Tess's original poems. She is a highly skilled botanical illustrator. Most of her cards are scientifically accurate drawings of flowers rendered with fine-tipped pens.

The first card he bought from her — *Crimson Columbine* — contained the following poem.

this wildflower
short-lived, yes,
but no prisoner

A few months later, he met Tess walking on Ocean Beach. They were both searching for unbroken sand dollars. He introduced himself and asked if he might hire her to make a drawing of the leaves and flowers of *camellia sinensis* — tea — for his business card and stationery. She was happy to make the drawing for him and he was thrilled with the result. Since then they have met every week for lunch.

"I made you something," she says, handing him a greeting card. "That's *Arnica mollis*. Cordilleran Arnica. I love how the yellow flower stands out against the dusky green leaves."

He opens the card.

> *Dear friend,*
> *Winter is nearly upon us.*
> *May I sleep on your sofa at night until Spring?*
> *I will be quieter than a mouse.*
> *I will leave no indentation.*
> *For the rest of my life,*
> *I will make drawings and poems for you.*
> *Blessings and Love,*
>   *Tess*

Idiot Compassion

Dorothy's heart is pounding. Here he is — the man who changed her life and saved her marriage. She is a Buddhist today because of his writings, his audiotapes, his clarity and honesty and humor — his inspiration. Darkly handsome, his father from Bangalore, his mother from Madras, he looks no older than forty, yet Dorothy knows he is sixty-two.

A favorite of movie stars and college students, posters of his beautiful face adorn countless walls around the world. And now *she* is about to drive him from San Francisco to a forest retreat in the wilds of Mendocino. They will be alone together, just the two of them, for five hours.

She looks down at her trembling hands and feels old and ungainly and unworthy of him, though she is a lovely woman of fifty, an accomplished yogini and a devoted practitioner of meditation.

He is moving through Customs garbed in a white long-sleeved shirt, black cotton trousers, and simple brown sandals. His glossy black hair is caught in a ponytail that falls to his waist. His baggage consists of a small wicker suitcase and a walnut walking stick exactly his height — five feet nine inches. And so effortless are his movements, he seems to be floating on air.

"Dorothy," he says, making his way through the throng to her, though she has yet to raise the sign identifying herself. "How kind of you to come fetch me."

He takes her hand and looks into her eyes and she bursts into tears, unable to contain her joy and amazement at finally meeting him. He engulfs her in a warm embrace and holds her as a father would hold a frightened child until she feels relieved enough to go on.

"I'm so sorry," she says, shyly taking the sky blue handkerchief he offers her. "I've just been *so* looking forward to meeting you. I can't tell you how important you are to me."

He bows. "As you are to me." He winks. "Now I must find a bathroom before I burst."

As she starts the engine of the red Mercedes — borrowed from her friend, Lisa, on the condition that she get Him to sign her copy of his bestseller *Why Not Smile?* — Dorothy clears her throat and says, "Is there anything you'd like to see or do in San Francisco before we head north?"

He closes his eyes and muses for a moment. "We might go to Union Square and see if anyone will listen to me talk about the illusion of separateness."

Dorothy stiffens. "*Should* we?" She swallows anxiously. "I mean, if you want to, of course, but you're so famous, you'll cause a riot."

"Oh," he says, considering this. "Then what would you like to do? It was just an idea."

"Oh, well," she says, flushing with shame. "I…I'm so sorry. I should never have presumed to…"

"Dorothy," he says, touching her hand. "You're taking this too seriously." He smiles radiantly. "When I was seventeen I heard a voice say, 'Share with others what you sense about existence.' So this is what I do. And as we travel together, why don't we share what comes to us to say? Yes?"

"Okay," she says, her fear of him dissolving in the soothing tone and cadence of his voice. "I'll try."

Despite her vow not to talk too much, Dorothy tells him the story of her life and how she came to Buddhism after seeing a documentary about his five-year walk from India to Paris. "And then," she says, pausing dramatically, "I read your book *Nobody Home* and I decided *not* to leave my husband."

He frowns. "I wonder why?"

"Well, the bodhisattva vow," she says, nodding enthusiastically. "The nobility and the…the beauty of sacrificing ourselves to make the other person happy, even if they're difficult, or in the case of Derek, truly awful."

"But this is not the bodhisattva vow." He frowns at the passing hills. "This is a misunderstanding of Buddha's teachings. And it has a name. Idiot compassion." He taps his forehead. "I must try to explain this more clearly in my next book. Indeed, I may call my next book *Beware Idiot Compassion*."

"Oh, but it's been good," she says, laughing nervously. "It's *all* practice, right?"

"Certainly," he says, smiling faintly. "Shall we stop and walk on the beach?"

"Derek is definitely toxic," she says, nodding rapidly. "It hasn't been easy."

They walk for a mile on windswept sand, the sun playing peek-a-boo through tattered clouds, the surf thunderous.

"Let us imagine," he says, gesturing toward the sea, "that I am a bodhisattva. What does that mean to you?"

Overwhelmed to be with him in such a wild place, Dorothy speaks falteringly, afraid to say the wrong thing. "You've attained enlightenment. But rather than step off the wheel of existence, you choose to stay for the benefit of others."

"What *specific* benefit?" he asks, fixing his eyes upon her.

"To aid them in their passage to enlightenment," she says, exultant to know the answer.

"Yes," he says, taking her hand. "But why would you interpret that as a directive to stay in an abusive marriage?"

"Because the idea is not to run away from difficulty, but to work through it." She gnaws on her lower lip. "Right?"

"Yes," he says, nodding gravely. "And have you worked through it with Derek?"

"No." She grimaces. "I...no."

"How long have you been married to him?"

"Eighteen years," she whispers. "But I've only been a Buddhist for nine."

He continues to nod slowly, composing his words before speaking. "My dear Dorothy, you are hiding behind an extremely shallow interpretation of the dharma. You are afraid to be alone. Your practice will never progress beyond superficiality until you remove yourself from the psychic imposition of this man. You are not serving his higher good or your own by perpetuating this relationship. And had I not said this to you, I, too, would have been guilty of idiot compassion."

The Edge

David strips the bed quickly, hoping to remove the sheets before any of Jonah's urine can soak into the mattress. David is a muscular man, his movements stiff and forceful. He sees no stain on the mattress cover. He touches the fabric with his hand. Dry. His shoulders relax. Now he won't have to drag the heavy mattress through the house and out onto the patio to dry. Nor will he have to set up the temporary bed in the living room.

Jonah, bent and withered, his skin hanging fabric-like on his bones, enters the room naked. "I'm so sorry," he murmurs. "God, I'm sorry to put you through this."

"It's no big deal," says David, swiftly making the bed with clean, dry sheets. "Didn't even soak through to the mattress. We'll lay down some towels. You'll be fine."

Jonah sits wearily on the edge of an armless chair. His breath is labored, his eyes barely open. "I will not be fine. I'm losing it, David. I'm wetting my bed now."

David flings the second blanket out over the bed — the bright yellow cloth billowing voluptuously before settling neatly atop the gray. "You're recovering from a debilitating illness," he says mechanically. "You are getting better. You are."

"That is a lie," says Jonah, too weak to shake his head. "I almost fainted just now coming back from the bathroom. I can't even lie down without your help."

David places two blue towels — one atop the other — on the sheet where Jonah's genitals will rest. "It's a good sign actually," he says, pulling Jonah to his feet. "You were finally sleeping deeply. That's when we do our best healing."

"I've heard," says Jonah, his legs trembling, "that for a few thousand dollars a certain pill may be bought. One pill containing everything we need to end this nightmare."

David lowers Jonah onto the bed and helps him settle against a mound of pillows. "Something to drink?" he asks, avoiding his old friend's eyes. "Tea?"

"Hemlock," says Jonah, swallowing dryly. "I'm serious, David. I don't want to go on like this."

"Can you give it another couple days before we discuss suicide?" David nods in support of himself. "Please?"

"But why?" asks Jonah, squeezing his eyes shut in response to a sharp pain in his gut. "Why prolong the suffering?"

"Because you *can* recover," says David, flushing with anger. "Dr. McKenzie says that…"

"Dr. McKenzie is not in my body," says Jonah, burning with fever. "I am not a generalization. I am dying, David. I asked you to help me. You said you would."

"I said I would help you with your recovery," says David, his heart pounding. "Not with your death."

"I see," says Jonah, using the last of his strength to throw off the covers. "Then you should go."

"Don't be absurd," says David, fiercely shaking his head. "I'll fix you some tea. It's time for another pain pill. You always feel hopeless when the pain…"

Jonah subsides into stillness. David turns away and takes a step toward the doorway. But something — an invisible hand on his shoulder — brings him back to the foot of the bed where for the first time in all the weeks he has been caring for Jonah, he opens himself to the possibility that this fine man will not recover; that the end of this body is imminent. And he realizes that he, David, is here to escort his mentor and friend to the edge of death — and there to wish him fond farewell.

Jonah opens his eyes and smiles at David exactly as he first smiled at him thirty years ago upon reading David's poem, the one ending with the words

and life shall intervene
to mask the sadder truths
with temporal joys —
for a time, yes, a time —
until our teacher calls us in from recess,
back into the schoolhouse.

FORGIVENESS

Diana is eight months pregnant. For several nights now she has dreamt of Jes, the man she left for Blair, her current husband. In all of these dreams, Jes is waiting for her — at a table in a café, on a bench in a park, on a rock beside a mountain path. She always wakes before she reaches him, though in her last dream she got close enough to hear him say, "I can't go on until you forgive me."

She tells her dream to Blair as they lie in bed together, their four hands on her great belly, communing with their baby.

Blair muses for a moment and says, "What do you need to forgive him for?"

"Nothing," she whispers. "I'm the one who did the cheating."

"Don't say that," says Blair, regretting his question. "It takes two to tango. I'm sure he had plenty of his own infidelities."

"No, honey." She shakes her head. "Not Jes."

"Look, we've been over this a thousand times," says Blair, too angry to stay in bed. "He's not a saint and you're not a sinner. That's old paradigm crap. We've evolved, remember? You stopped loving him and you started loving me. There's no shame in that."

"I know," she says, remembering how Jes always brought her tea in bed to start the day, how he would gaze at her for a long time in the morning light, loving her. "I think I'll go see him today. This makes seven nights in a row I've dreamt of him."

"He's a *monk* now," says Blair, storming into the bathroom. "Why bother?"

"Because," she says to the slamming door, "I want him to forgive *me* before I have this baby."

When Jes entered the rural monastery following the demise of his relationship with Diana, he was drawn inexorably to the kitchen. And now, two years gone by, he is head chef, much to the joy of his community and to the growing number of visitors who travel there to taste his delectable creations.

Diana arrives in time for lunch, and knowing nothing of Jes's culinary ascendancy, she enters the cafeteria expecting to find him among the diners. When she doesn't see him at any of the tables, she inquires of a young man serving rice if he knows where Jes is.

"He's in the kitchen," says the young man, smiling at her. "Are you Diana?"

She blushes. "Yes. Could you tell him I'm here?"

The young man disappears through the swinging door. When Jes emerges a moment later, covered from head to toe in white flour, he is greeted by a ripple of applause from the happy diners — an elderly monk shouting, "Bravo, Jes! Bravo!"

Jes embraces Diana and laughs, "Can you believe this? I'm a cook now."

On the edge of the sprawling garden, Jes and Diana sit side by side on a bench beneath a weeping willow. In the distance, a monk and a nun wearing broad-brimmed straw hats move slowly along rows of young cabbage plants, hoeing the rampant weeds.

To the west, a rust-red hawk — her downy white legs dangling beneath her — circles low over a meadow of wild grasses.

Diana places Jes's hand on her big round belly. The baby kicks. Jes feels the percussion in the palm of his hand. His eyes fill with tears. Diana puts her arms around him and they weep together.

DEATH

Kenny, three years old — blond and tall for his age — watches a bee probing a blossom on a raspberry bush. Kenny's grandfather, Tom, a broad-shouldered man with a full head of white hair, stands nearby, half-watching his grandson and half-looking toward his house.

Tom's eyes are red from weeping. Jeanine, his wife of forty-four years, died during the night. His daughter, Carol, Kenny's mother, is inside overseeing the removal of the body to the funeral home.

"Can I kill it?" asks Kenny, frowning at the bee as it withdraws from the flower and flies to the next lucky bloom.

"What?" says Tom, on the verge of tears again. "What did you say, Kenny?"

"Can I kill it?" He glares at his grandfather. "The bee?"

"No, no," says Tom, moving to Kenny's side. "Bees are good. You know what he's doing?"

"No," says Kenny, pouting. "Bees sting you."

"Only if you bother them." Tom kneels on the gravel path that wends its way through the verdant garden of flowers and fruit trees — Jeanine's garden. "You see that yellow stuff on his legs?" He points to the blobs of pollen coating the bee's legs. "Every time he goes into a flower, some of that rubs off and tells the flower to make a berry. If we didn't have bees we wouldn't have any food to eat."

Kenny shrugs. "I hate bees."

"No, you don't," says Tom, rising with a grunt. "If you love food, you love bees."

"What if I only killed *one*?" Kenny raises his stick to make a swipe at the bee.

"No!" says Tom, snatching the stick from Kenny and snapping it in two. "I told you to leave the bees alone."

Kenny bursts into tears. "Mommy! Mommy! He broke my sword. My best sword."

"I'll make you another one." Tom holds out his hand to Kenny. "An even better one."

"No!" cries Kenny, sobbing convulsively. "Never!"

While Carol puts Kenny to bed upstairs, Tom does the dinner dishes as he has every night for forty-four years. He and Jeanine divided the labors of their marriage in ways that pleased them both. He cooked breakfast, she did the morning dishes. She cooked supper, he did the evening dishes and swept the kitchen. She dusted, he vacuumed. He did the heavier work in the garden — digging, pruning, lifting — and she did the planting, weeding, and watering. She made their bed every morning, he did the grocery shopping. She went to church, he played golf.

They did many things together, too. They loved to go camping, and they saw every movie that came to the neighborhood cinema, except the violent ones. And every Saturday morning, rain permitting, they would have tea and freshly baked cookies under the big blue umbrella in the center of the garden. This was when they would never fail to ask each other how they were feeling and what they were thinking about.

Now she is gone — his best friend and lover of forty-four years. Gone.

He puts the broom and dustpan away and takes down the flashlight to light his way as he searches for slugs and snails and earwigs feeding on the plants in Jeanine's garden.

He goes first to the new bed of lettuce, the last plants Jeanine set into the ground before she died. He was there when she lowered the dangling roots of the seedlings into the holes she'd scooped in the pliable soil.

"You did such a good job, Tom," she said, her cheeks dimpling as she gazed up at him. "So soft and rich this year."

"I love you," he says, illuminating a shiny path of goo leading to the base of a spindly seedling.

He kneels down and picks a slug off the baby lettuce, crushing the mollusk between his thumb and fingers — remembering his wife.

THE DHARMA OF
EXPERIENCE

On a warm day in October, Gerald sits at his desk composing a letter to his wife. They have been married for eighteen years and he has never — until now — suspected her of being unfaithful to him.

> *Tina,*
> *I have just received a letter from Dean detailing your various love affairs.*

Gerald shakes his head and begins anew.

> *Dear Tina,*
> *Dean has written to me. He claims that you and he have been lovers for the past fifteen years. He further claims that you and Frank have been lovers since before our wedding, and that Ellen has been your lover for nine years.*

Gerald puts down his pen and rubs his eyes. He feels oddly detached, as if he's in a play he has little interest in.

> *Tina,*
> *Why would you go to such lengths to deceive me?*

We were in therapy for seven years together.
Was it all a charade for you?
Have you ever told me the truth?

Bessie, a fat old golden retriever with rheumy eyes and a black tongue, waddles into the room with a leash in her mouth. She whimpers politely and wags her tail.

Gerald frowns at her and asks, "How could I have not known?"

Walking Bessie along a quiet lane, Gerald suddenly feels dizzy. He drops the leash and allows his dog to walk on without him. He kneels on the sidewalk, the earth tilting and spinning. He lies on his back and closes his eyes.

Dusk gives way to darkness. Tina sits on the sofa sipping a cup of chamomile tea. A cold wind howls through the eucalyptus grove and buffets the house. Gerald squats on the hearth, building a fire.

"You're so good at that," she says softly. "I love how easy it is for you to get the wood to catch."

Gerald turns to her. "You must have said that to me a thousand times. And it always makes me feel good."

"Well, I love you," she says simply. "Are you okay? You seem distant tonight."

He adds a big log to the fire and takes his customary place beside her on the sofa. Bessie lies at their feet as she always does in the evenings when they sit together in front of the fire. The phone rings four times and falls silent. The flames lap at the log, consuming it quickly.

"I'm okay," says Gerald, remembering what he saw when the dizziness passed and he opened his eyes.

a hawk
riding invisible currents
in a cloudless sky

Karma

Matthew lives in a coastal village some two hundred miles north of San Francisco. He owns his house outright — a seven-acre farm bought with all but a few of the dollars he inherited from his mother. He grows vegetables, herbs, and flowers in his sprawling garden, and his orchard provides him with copious quantities of fruit. A flock of chickens and ducks supplies him with eggs and meat, and his spring-fed pond teems with trout.

He earns what little money he requires by working two days a week in the town's only bookstore, and by pruning fruit trees. He is a voracious reader of short stories, a prodigious letter writer, and a cat lover — he owns three and feeds several others. His one vice, as he laughingly refers to it, is a thirst for good tea, notably Dragonwell.

Three times a year, Matthew travels to San Francisco, his former home, to purchase tea and to commune with his brilliant friend Karl. He usually stays for two or three days, catches a foreign movie, and makes the rounds of used bookstores in search of short story collections.

He has been a bachelor for the last fourteen of his fifty-six years. Living alone — with only occasional visits from friends — no longer saddens him. He attributes this gradual cessation of sorrow to his daily practice of meditation, prayer, and study of the dharma. He still imagines entering into a lasting relationship with a woman, but since the finale of his only marriage, his romantic liaisons have been few and difficult and brief.

Matthew's friends wonder about his lack of love partners, for he is a charming man of great warmth and sensitivity. Once, when asked why he has been single for so long, he replied, "Maybe I was an unfaithful cad in a previous life and I'm paying for that now. But it probably has more to do with my fear of being told yet again that I'm not good enough."

As he becomes more and more attuned to the pleasures of his rural existence, he feels less and less inclined to make the long trek to San Francisco. He is quite certain that if not for his friend, Karl, he might never undertake the journey again.

And so on a sunny day in February, Matthew arrives at Karl's flat on Russian Hill, tired from his long journey on a crowded bus. But when he rings the bell, Karl only opens his door a crack to say, "Can't happen. I've met a woman. She'll be here any minute. You understand."

"Actually, I don't," says Matthew, frowning at his friend. "I've come a long way, Karl. I'm exhausted. We confirmed all this day before yesterday. I wouldn't have come if…"

"Not possible," shouts Karl. "I've been after this one for a long time. I don't want to blow it now."

"But Karl…"

"No," he says, slamming the door.

Matthew is so shocked by this turn of events that he remains frozen in place for several minutes, wondering if this is some sort of incredibly lucid dream. Surely he didn't imagine Karl saying, "Six on the dot. Can't wait to see you. I've cleared the boards for three days so we shall not be interrupted."

Now a woman's voice rouses Matthew from his stupor.

"I'm here to see Karl?" she says, smiling timidly. "Are you a friend of his?"

"No," says Matthew, hoisting his pack onto his back and striding away.

In the depths of Chinatown, Matthew sits at a rickety table in a garish Chinese restaurant, eating a bowl of noodles and wondering how best to proceed. He has two hundred dollars — a hundred for tea, twenty for books, and eighty for treating Karl to inexpensive meals.

But now — after he finds a few books and some good green tea — he wishes only to catch the next bus for home.

In the shop where he has purchased tea for the last fifteen years, Matthew is greeted by Mr. Yee, an elderly man in a plain brown suit with an incongruous pink bow tie. "Four month now since you came before," says Mr. Yee, nodding and smiling.

Matthew buys fourteen ounces of fine Dragonwell, and is about to say goodbye when Mr. Yee asks, "Please to try new Bi Luo Chun? So delicate. Very good. Delicious. You be surprise."

They sit at a dark teak table in a corner of the cluttered

shop — Mr. Yee's yellow canary hopping around in the bamboo cage above them. Mr. Yee drops a pinch of tiny curled leaves into a small white teapot full of tepid water.

"*So* delicate," he says, watching the leaves unfurl. "Water too hot, tea no good."

They drink the divine ephemera and Matthew feels filled to the brim with blessings.

❀

A year later, Matthew receives a letter from Karl.

Dear Matthew,

I infer from your long silence that you must be angry with me. You know perfectly well how irrational I become when I'm about to have sex. Your timing couldn't have been worse. You should have waited a few hours and called. As it happened, things didn't work out with that particular female, and I was gravely disappointed not to have a visit with you.

Not to worry. I will travel to you. All I lack is the money for such an extensive adventure. I'm hoping you will be generous enough to send me three hundred dollars as I am perilously low on funds. I am owed several thousand but the bastards won't pay.

Please don't hold a grudge. I miss you. No one else understands me half as well as you do. I'm so looking forward to seeing your Eden. I've wanted to come for years now, but one thing or another always intervenes.

I can't wait to hear from you. Write soon.

As always,

Karl

Matthew reads Karl's letter twice, and after a long walk on the beach, makes his reply.

Dear Karl,

I certainly had my moments of feeling angry about being rebuffed by you, but in the larger scheme of my life, I now see that what happened at your door was beneficial — a significant turning point.

I was no longer happy making that exhausting trip to San Francisco, and as I said to you then, I would not have made the trip if I couldn't stay with you. Being told to go away by someone as important to me as you were supplied the impetus for me to fully disengage from my past there and enter more completely into my life here. I no longer need to venture south in quest of tea. Mr. Yee, knowing my predilections, now sends me generous samples from which I order my stock.

The apple trees are blossoming madly, the honeybees hard at work, my cats enjoying these warmer nights. I have been reading Maupassant again — such a genius. I, too, am currently low on funds. My hours at the bookstore have been reduced to one day a week, and no

*one hereabouts likes to have their trees pruned when
they are blooming so spectacularly.*
   Blessings and Love,
     Matthew

AGGRESSION

Chucho and Camille were littermates, but as full-grown dogs they do not resemble each other in the least. Chucho is a big heavy male with a barrel chest and short black hair — very much a water dog. Camille is slightly taller than Chucho, but slender and brown and longhaired and wholly disinterested in water. On those rare nights when the temperature falls below freezing, Chucho reluctantly comes inside the house to sleep; otherwise he is to be found out of doors. Camille prefers life on the plush sofa in front of the fire.

Chucho always rides in the bed of the pickup, rain or shine, reveling in the chilly breeze off his beloved ocean. Camille will occasionally deign to ride in her master's truck, but only on the non-negotiable condition that she sit beside him in the cab. Chucho only rests when he is too exhausted to take another step, whereas Camille doesn't seem to have a restless bone in her body. Yet they have the same mother — a purebred Dalmatian.

Only when their food is served — morning and evening — do Camille and Chucho meet to exchange cordial licks before eating from their separate bowls. Chucho devours his mountain of food in a few ravenous gulps before dashing out the door to resume his patrol of the woods, while Camille eats slowly and daintily before returning to her sofa.

These unlikely siblings have not grappled since puppyhood,

and if life were static, their peaceful coexistence might never be disturbed.

The humans in the mix are a large man named Tony, a former anthropology professor, and Maria, a former elementary school teacher. Tony supplies firewood to rustic inns and vacation homes that abound in the vicinity of their forest cottage. He gets the wood by clearing logging residue from coastal creeks. Maria is an herbalist and midwife. She gathers her herbs in the wilds and from their deer-fenced garden.

One foggy morning in August, Tony leaves Maria slumbering in their bed and wanders to the kitchen to feed the dogs. Hearing Tony padding down the hallway, Camille leaves her bed by the fallen fire and traipses after him. To their mutual surprise, Chucho does not come barging through the dog door, as is his custom upon hearing the rustling of the food bags.

Tony fills Camille's bowl with fine kibble imported from France, and goes outside to see what Chucho is up to. Camille is so distracted by her brother's uncharacteristic absence at breakfast that she exits through the dog door — an extremely rare occurrence — to see where her brother is.

As she steps onto the porch, Camille spots Chucho emerging from the woods with what appears to be a large gray sausage held tenderly in his mouth. The sausage whimpers. Camille growls, recognizing the thing to be a newborn puppy.

"It's okay, Sweetie," says Tony, turning to smile at Camille. "He's just a little baby. Nothing to be afraid of."

Camille's wolfish eyes narrow and she growls again before going back inside. She disdains her food and retreats to her sofa where she lies down and covers her eyes with her paws.

Having delivered the pup into Tony's hands, Chucho rambles into the house, finds his bowl empty, gobbles Camille's kibble, slurps a quart of water, and rushes back outside.

Maria is filling an eyedropper with warm milk for the ravenous newborn when Chucho enters with another pup in his mouth, this one dead.

Maria raises an eyebrow and says to Tony, "I think our hero has found a litter in the creek."

While Tony goes to get his shovel, Maria swaddles the living pup in a wool sweater and sets him in a cardboard box on the kitchen table. She wraps the dead pup in an old bandana, and places the shrouded corpse in her knapsack.

The humans follow Chucho through a forest of young redwoods and ascend a deer trail beside a nameless creek that swells to roaring when the rains come. In a shallow pool where the creek crosses a meadow, they find seven little corpses in a burlap sack weighed down with river rocks — three more bodies loose in the water — the litter so recently drowned, the ravens have yet to discover the carrion.

Knowing Chucho will eventually bring home all the dead babies if allowed to, the humans bury the bodies in a deep hole and place four boulders atop the grave to discourage Chucho from digging them up.

As they come in sight of their house, Chucho bolts ahead of the humans and crashes through the dog door to do battle with Camille — the humans arriving just in time to separate the snarling dogs before they can seriously injure each other.

The cardboard box stands upside down on the floor — a fortuitous landing that saved the tiny passenger from Camille's murderous jaws.

"Bad girl," says Maria, shaking a finger at Camille. "That little baby can't hurt you."

"Please don't yell at her," says Tony, intervening. "I think I can explain this to her."

Cradling the pup against his tummy, Tony sits on the sofa with Camille and pets her with his free hand, while Chucho straddles the threshold between the kitchen and the living room, watching Camille and listening intently to Tony.

"Here's the thing," says Tony, scratching Camille's ears — her favorite place to be touched. "I understand you're upset about having a new dog in the family. Everything happened so suddenly. We didn't give you any time to get used to the idea. Maybe you think this puppy will get in the way of our loving you. But if that happens, I promise we'll find the puppy some other place to live. Because we want you to be happy, Camille. We love you. You know that. So what we'd like is for you to give this little guy a chance. You don't have to do anything special. You don't have to change the way you do things. Just don't hurt him, okay? Because he's important to Chucho. And he's important to us, too. So I'm asking you, as my very best friend, to be kind to the pup and not hurt him. Okay?"

Tony offers the newborn to Camille. She sniffs at the pup and gently licks his tiny body.

Now Chucho joins them, wagging his tail and licking the puppy, and licking Camille, too, as Maria comes in from the kitchen, smiling radiantly.

CELIBACY

"But don't you miss sex?" she asks, intensely aroused by his disinterest in her. "You always enjoyed it so much."

"My obsession with sex was a gigantic obstacle to ever actually being here." He smiles fondly at her. "In fact, I'm pretty sure it was *the* obstacle."

"But you're still so young." She undresses him with her eyes. "You're in such great shape. How can you stand it?"

"I was miserable," he says, turning off the whistling kettle. "I'm actually pretty happy now, and I remind myself of that whenever I feel the old compulsions arising."

"But do you…" She blushes. "Do yourself?"

"No." He refreshes their cups. "Though I occasionally have erotic dreams that result in fruition."

"But what's the point?" She closes her eyes and imagines him naked. "It seems like such a waste of your fantastic potential. I mean, there are armies of desperate women out there looking for a decent man. And I'm one of them now."

He opens his window a crack to admit the winter air — the cabin suddenly hot. "I don't recall your feeling that my potential was being wasted. In fact, what I remember most was your contempt for my sexual appetite." He gazes out at the gentle rain. "I suppose I might have considered celibacy a waste if anyone had ever really wanted me. But no one ever did. Not for long."

"You mean this isn't some sort of spiritual choice? You're doing this because you can't get the women you want and can't keep the ones you get?"

"How unkind of you," he says, sadly surprised. "I didn't expect this from you."

"What did you expect? That I'd apologize for teasing you? For promising and promising and never delivering?"

"No," he says, shaking his head. "I expected you'd be curious about my decision and then glad to know I was feeling so much better, not so desperate, not so afraid of being alone."

"I *was* horrible to you." She moves closer. "I tortured you because I hated myself. But now I don't."

He sets his teacup down and enfolds her in a warm embrace. "We did the best we could. We were trying to kill our pain with sex instead of facing the deeper causes of our anguish."

"You're turning me on," she whispers, kissing his throat. "God, I want you."

"I'm sorry," he says, releasing her. "I'm done with that."

"You're just teasing me," she says, hot and angry. "Taking your revenge."

"No. This is how I wish to live now."

"Oh come on." She presses against him and thrusts her hands under his shirt. "You know you want me."

"I am learning to love without yearning for sex," he says, taking a deep breath. "Without yearning for anything."

IGNORANCE

The earwigs are a plague on the garden.

Jonathon — a thickset man with an unruly gray beard — wanders up and down the rows of decimated bean plants searching for surviving leaves, finding none. How curious, and what a disaster for the community. He has been gardening for fifty years, since he was six years old, and he has never experienced such an infestation — nothing even close to this. Only the garlic shoots have weathered the onslaught of the ravenous bugs, and even they show signs of being nibbled.

Having tea with Malcolm, his predecessor at the helm of the abbey garden, Jonathon says, "I went out last night at midnight and there were thousands and thousands of earwigs clinging to every stem and leaf. I've scoured the garden for their nests, but except for one small concentration near the old greenhouse..."

Malcolm, eighty-seven, a slender man with boyish dimples, shakes his head. "You won't find concentrations." He swirls the tea in his cup to bring out a last burst of flavor from the leaves. "They're everywhere in the ground."

"But why this year?" Jonathon gazes at the slice of garden he can see through Malcolm's open door. "There's nothing much different about the weather this spring than last. Our methods haven't changed."

Malcolm settles back in his rocking chair, a smile playing at his lips. "I must tell you, I'm glad it's not my worry now. I'd be out there all night picking the buggers off one by one."

"But what do you think it is?" Jonathon frowns at what he can see of the ruined planting. "We'll have to start over again. And we'll have to *buy* vegetables this year. I feel like such a fool." He turns to Malcolm. "Can you make a guess?"

"No need to guess," says Malcolm, finishing his tea. "The same thing happened to me my third year here — forty-four, no, forty-five years ago. And ever after we always dug the compost in deep and never top dressed with young compost that had any wood chips or sawdust in it. That's just elixir to an earwig."

"Oh, my God," says Jonathon — awareness dawning in his tired eyes. "The sawdust we got from the mill in January and mixed with the manure."

"Yes, and you have five new apprentices who don't know how to thoroughly rake the clods out of the new beds. Those warm little pockets under the clods are perfect boudoirs for earwig orgies." Malcolm rocks forward and rises from his chair. "But even so, you might not have had this plague if there'd been a good freeze this winter to kill off most of their eggs, but it never got terribly cold."

Jonathon stares in amazement at Malcolm. "How long have you known?"

"All along," he says, stepping into his garden clogs.

"And you didn't say anything because I told you not to butt

in anymore." He closes his eyes and shakes his head. "I'm such an idiot."

"No, no," says Malcolm, putting a hand on Jonathon's shoulder. "You're a fine gardener. We can't know everything."

"So what did you do back then to kill them off? Poison?"

"Never." Malcolm laughs as he steps outside his cottage — his sinecure for fifty years of service to the sangha. "What we did was double-dig the ground and make the new garden immaculate. Then we sunk big bowls every six feet along the rows and filled them with beer. Earwigs love beer even more than they love baby basil. That drowned a good many of them, and we were out every night for two weeks picking the rest of the buggers off by hand until the plants were strong enough to fend for themselves."

"I guess that's what we'll have to do," says Jonathon, relieved to have the mystery solved, however difficult the remedy.

"Have you seen *my* little vegetable patch?" asks Malcolm, starting up a narrow trail leading away from the main garden. "Up in the old orchard?"

"I didn't know you'd planted anything this year," says Jonathon, watching him go. "I've been so busy with the expansion of the fields, and the master classes, and…"

"I've been fortunate." Malcolm beckons him to follow. "Not many bugs up there. Might get enough beans and such to see us through until yours come ready. Come on. I'll show you."

CRISIS

The rustic cottage at Quail Valley zendo is a single large room containing kitchen, living room, bedroom, and bathroom. Sheltered by two massive oaks, the little house overlooks Coyote Gulch, a ravine carved by a stream that only flows in the immediate aftermath of rain.

Theodore, fifty-six, a gregarious poet and counselor, was the sole occupant of the house for three years prior to the very recent arrival of Elise, fifty-two, a former fashion model and San Francisco socialite. They have known each other for ten years, and though very much in love for all that time, they were not lovers until three weeks ago — their mutual celibacy ending on their first night in bed together, a December tempest raging — longtime soloists suddenly living in close quarters.

Having given up the pampered life of a millionaire's wife to become the partner of a penniless Buddhist poet, and having dedicated the last three years to the study and practice of Buddhism, Elise is absolutely certain she is precisely where God intends her to be.

Theodore, on the other hand, is by turns elated and desperately uncomfortable to have Elise so undeniably present in his life. Living alone, despite painful bouts of loneliness, was child's play for Theodore compared to sharing his intimate space — day in and day out — with another person. That is why he has volunteered for an extra shift in the community garden and undertaken a Herculean reorganization of the zendo library.

"Love," posits Roshi Takayanagi, "has filled our Theo with a passion to serve."

Yet Theodore knows perfectly well that his seeming passion for service is nothing more than a futile attempt to avoid the inevitable — telling Elise he made a terrible mistake by inviting her to live with him.

For the first time in twenty years, Theodore craves alcohol. When he sits in meditation now, his mind plays vivid movies of him walking into bars and downing shots of whiskey. His daily walk, previously a four-mile jaunt along gently sloping pathways, has become a twelve-mile forced march up and down the steepest trails — all in an effort to exhaust himself so he will be less susceptible to the killing tension in being alone with Elise.

Elise sits in her rocking chair, gazing at the fire. Their cat, Charlie, a big gray tabby, sits on Elise's lap, delighted by the absentminded caresses of the new human.

Rain clouds have blotted out the moonlight. The room is deliciously warm, lit only by the flickering flames. Elise smiles in anticipation of Theodore's arrival. He has kitchen duty and so will be another little while before ascending the path from the dining hall to their cottage.

She opens her journal and writes:

I rose at 4:30 this morning and started the fire, then went back to bed and snuggled with Theo until the house was warm. His mind was so far away I might have been holding a big, sweet, brainless body. He's having a difficult time with my being here, though I think his struggle is less about me than about sharing his space, physical and psychic, with anyone. He stayed in bed watching me while I stretched before I left for the morning sitting. He said he was too tired to get up, but I'm sure he jumped out of bed the minute I walked out the door. He is programmed to live alone.

Pained by thoughts of Theodore's discomfort, she puts down her pen and rolls her shoulders. She wants to help him, yet she knows the transition from living apart to living together will not always be easy. She sought advice from Roshi Takayanagi about how to assist Theodore in overcoming his resistance to sharing time and space with her.

The wiry old man held out his hands, palms up, and said, "Patience, humor, compassion. Mix and match."

Theodore comes in from the cold, his arms full of firewood, his cheeks rosy, his hair blown wild by the wind. Elise watches him keenly, loving how easy it is to be silent with him — to commune without words. He stokes the fire and opens the window over their bed an inch to let in fresh air. He takes off his jacket and hangs it in the closet they share. He caresses her shoulder on his way to fill the kettle for tea.

She wants to say something to relieve his anguish, but resists the urge — her thoughts coming and going, none alighting.

Theodore squats by the fire, wondering how best to tell her that he is too old to make the adjustment from being alone for twenty-five years to being with her in such an intense sexual partnership. *I will move into the dormitory if you wish to remain in the community. I love you too much. I...I love you too much.*

He sits in the armchair beside her and picks up a dog-eared copy of *Buddha's Sister* by the teacher Ina. He opens the book at random, his eyes drawn to a paragraph that begins, "So this, I realized, was to be an essential element of my practice..."

"Read to me," says Elise, nodding to her beloved.

Theodore clears his throat. "So this, I realized, was to be an essential element of my practice, untangling the knots of old words and phrases that bound me to a self-destructive idea of who and what I am."

He pauses, considering the phrases *I love you too much*, *I'm too old*, *This isn't working*, and sees himself trapped in a net of ridiculous ideas.

"Go on," she urges, knowing the passage by heart.

"I saw that I depended on fear to define myself, that I had developed a mistrust of change. I understood Buddha's most courageous act was to rid himself of any expectation of outcome — trusting completely in the exquisite resiliency and creativity of the soul. Life can be a marvelous improvisation, whether we play alone, in duet, in trio, quartet, or with ten thousand other singers and thinkers and lovers of this life, this breath, this divine chance to see what happens."

Theodore looks up from the page, the denseness of his worry lessened by reading these words aloud. Here is Elise, a woman, a person, a concentration of matter illuminated by a vibrant spirit, happy to be with him.

"I'm hanging by a thread," he murmurs, closing the book.

"Let go," she whispers. "Let go, Theo."

"But then I'll fall." He frowns at her. "And I may drink again."

"So fall and drink." Her eyes meet his. "But first talk to me, and trust me."

"I trust you," he says meekly.

"Do you?" She rises to serve their tea. "Maybe you don't trust anyone because you were so terribly abused by your parents. Maybe that's why you drank. Maybe that's why you chose to live alone, because you only trusted yourself."

He forces a laugh. "Oh, that's too obvious."

"Obvious means clear," she says, handing him a steaming cup. "As long as I was on my way here, your pattern of aloneness was yet to be interrupted. You could fantasize in the safety of being alone. But now I'm here. And what is the *only* thing that has ever happened to you in relationship?"

"Elise," he says, shaking his head, "I don't want to belittle your psychological insight, but I'm sure that's not it."

"What is not it?" she asks, wanting to shake him.

"That I'm afraid you'll abandon me." He shrugs painfully. "It's much more likely *I'll* run away."

She nods. "In either case, we'll break apart."

"I'm sorry," he says, his shame mastering him. "I feel horrible about enticing you here."

"*You* enticed *me*?" She laughs her sparkling laugh. "Oh, Theo, your ego is running rampant through the zendo."

"Stop it," he says, pouting. "It's not a matter of ego. I'm talking about the fact that you gave up everything for me and I don't measure up."

"You fit me to perfection," she says, standing behind him and resting her hands on his shoulders. "I never dreamed sex could be so good."

"You're impossible." He smiles despite himself. "I'm trying to tell you how I'm feeling."

"I know," she says, cradling his head against her tummy. "But before you say anything more, I want you to know I'm not going anywhere."

"Ever?" he asks, sounding just like a little boy begging his mother for love.

INTEGRITY

Lacking money for a taxi, Brandon — a boyish man, fifty-two, with close-cropped gray hair — walks the three miles from the train station to his father's mansion, fighting a powerful headwind. He ascends the steep driveway to the hilltop from where the great house commands a spectacular view of the megalopolis sprawling to the far horizons. His father's silver Rolls Royce gleams in the twilight. His sister's jade-green Jaguar is there, too, along with several other shiny new cars belonging to his stepmother and her children.

As Brandon approaches the broad stairway leading up to his father's massive front door, a dozen ravens descend from the cloudless sky and settle at the top of a towering eucalyptus — the slender boughs bending under the weight of the birds.

Brandon turns away from the house, not yet ready to face his family. He enters the expansive rose garden where a few stalwart blooms cling to their bushes in defiance of a freezing November. He sits wearily on an elegant teak bench beside a reflection pond surrounded by Japanese maples — some red, some green, some golden. He closes his eyes and recites a litany of affirmations known as *brahmaviharas*.

May I be free of fear.
May I be free of worry.
May I know physical well-being.
May I know mental well-being.
May I know emotional well-being.
May I know the ease of well-being.
May I know the grace of well-being.
May I be loved.
May I be supported.
May my happiness continue.
May my suffering be at end.
I am the owner of my own karma.
My happiness and unhappiness
depend on my actions.

Brandon rises from the bench and approaches the pond. A breeze ripples the water, blurring his image. He closes his eyes and begins the *brahmaviharas* again, changing the pronoun as he thinks of his father and sister.

May you be free of fear.
May you be free of worry.
May you know physical well-being.
May you know mental well-being.
May you know emotional well-being.
May you know the ease of well-being.
May you know the grace of well-being.

May you be loved.
May you be supported.
May your happiness continue.
May your suffering be at end.
You are the owner of your own karma.
Your happiness and unhappiness
depend on your actions.

Brandon raises his eyes to the upper branches of the eucalyptus, the shimmering leaves turning pink in the last light of day. The ravens cling to the slender boughs as they sway in a wind from the north.

Brandon has almost no money. He lives alone in a small room in a dangerous part of the city. He makes his living as the janitor of the theological school where he meditates for several hours every day. He only comes to his father's house one day each year — Thanksgiving. He has no other contact with his father and sister and their families.

"It's late," he says, watching the eucalyptus leaves turn from pink to gray. "They'll want to eat soon."

Still he does not rise. The knowledge of what will happen when he enters his father's house pins him down with the gravity of Jupiter.

If he climbs those stairs and opens that door, he will force himself to feign interest in the lives of people he barely knows, and they, knowing of his poverty, will not inquire about his life. His sister will show him photo albums documenting her recent travels abroad. His father will get very drunk and berate him for not traveling to Europe, for not marrying, for pissing his life away. Brandon will make no attempt to defend himself.

After supper, his sister will drive him to the train station. He will thank her for the ride. She will hand him an envelope and say, "Happy Holidays." There will be two checks in the envelope, one from his sister for five hundred dollars, one from his father for a thousand.

The ravens detach themselves from the branches and fly away to the west, murmuring to one another. As Brandon watches the birds become black dots above the silver horizon, he admits to himself that his sole motive for coming to his father's house is to get those checks from his sister. He does not make enough money as a janitor to cover his living expenses, but by being impeccably frugal, the gifts from his father and sister allow him to continue his studies and practice without other sources of income.

"I won't do this anymore," he says, rising from the bench and descending the hill through growing darkness.

A LIFE OF BUDDHA

A corpulent man of seventy-six, Jason is humming an advertising jingle as he opens the mailbox and brings forth a bundle of bills and magazines and…

He blinks in disbelief at an envelope bearing the unmistakable handwriting of his daughter Gina. They — Jason and his wife, Gloria — haven't heard a word from Gina in twenty-five years. They assumed she was dead.

Gloria — her girlish figure and surgically sculpted face belying her sixty-three years — is in the kitchen watching a talk show on television while she finishes her kelp and kefir smoothie. She is about to rush off to have sex with Hal. Jason thinks she's going to play bridge at the senior center. On Monday and Wednesday and Saturday Jason thinks Gloria is attending meetings of her garden club when she's actually in bed with her other lover Michael.

Gloria dries her hands, chases the kelp and kefir taste out of her mouth with a big gulp of coffee, grabs her purse, and dashes out the front door. To her surprise, Jason is not in his study staring at his computer screen but sitting on the front steps reading a letter and weeping.

"What happened?" she asks, never once having seen him cry in their forty-four years together.

"Gina," he says gruffly. "It's from Gina."

"Oh, my God," says Gloria, sitting beside him and putting a hand on his arm. "Where is she?"

"She's coming to see us." He looks at his wife's hand on him — the first time she's touched him in decades. "Today."

"*Today*?" She takes her hand away and thinks of how wild she and Hal have been for each other lately. "I'd better go to the store. We're low on everything." She jumps to her feet. "I wish she'd given us more notice."

"Postmarked a week ago." His fingers caress the envelope. "Wrong Zip Code."

"Doesn't surprise me," says Gloria, racing to her car. "I'll be back."

Jason fills a coffee mug with gin and downs the booze in a single gulp. Thus primed, he uncorks a bottle of red wine and walks through the house drinking directly from the bottle. Unconscious of his transit, he stands in the backyard, the wine bottle empty, his daughter's letter crumpled in his hand.

With a painful effort, he lowers himself onto a plastic chaise longue beside the neglected swimming pool — the water dense with algae — and wonders why he doesn't feel the least bit drunk. His stomach gurgles plaintively, and across the chasm of years he hears himself saying to Gina, "You're nothing but a filthy whore. I wish you were dead."

He uncrumples the letter and reads it again.

Dear Mother and Father,

I have just returned from a pilgrimage to Tibet.
Before I return to my home in California, I will be
giving talks in New York and Philadelphia, and one at
the theological school at Harvard, which means I'll only
be an hour's train ride from you. I would very much like
to visit you.

My name is now Ina and I am a horticulturist and a
writer. I live in a Buddhist community with my husband,
John, and our children Leo and Viva. Leo is twenty-
three, Viva is nineteen. Shortly after Viva's last birthday,
I fell into a severe depression. After several weeks of
misery, I determined the cause of my suffering was
my attachment to you and the events surrounding our
parting shortly after I turned nineteen.

I will call before traveling to see you. If you would
rather I did not come, I won't, though I think a reunion
would be beneficial for all of us.

With blessings and love,
Ina

Later in the day, his sense of time blurred by drunkenness, Jason picks up a ringing phone and has a brief conversation with his long lost daughter. He does not hear a word she says to him. He is only aware of her tone — a clear musical sound unlike anything he remembers about her.

He says, "No," whenever she falls silent, and finally, terrified by her calm persistence, he shouts, "Absolutely not!" and hangs up.

With trembling hands, he pours himself a glass of wine and sits on the sofa in the family room, saying over and over, "That was the best thing to do. That was necessary. Necessary."

Jason is watching a golf tournament on the big-screen television when Gloria's car pulls into the garage. He turns off the television. Gloria enters with two bulging bags of groceries.

"There are three more in the car," she says breathlessly.

"Where were you?" he asks, grunting with the effort of rising. "You left at ten. It's almost six."

"Did she call?" asks Gloria, ignoring his question. "When will she be here?"

"She's not coming." He nods to affirm this. "I told her not to come. I told her I didn't think it would do any good. I told her we were too old for this kind of thing."

"Oh, you angel!" says Gloria, giving him a peck on the cheek. "I was hoping and praying this would happen. That's the *real* reason I'm late. We just don't *need* this, do we? We've been through more than enough because of her."

"I'll get the groceries," he says, shuffling past her. "Open some wine why don't you?"

"Champagne!" she shouts as he disappears into the garage. "I'm gonna take a quick shower. Been running around in the heat all day."

In her shower, washing away the scent of her lover, Gloria says to the roaring water, "She's not his daughter anyway."

❖

Ina walks to the microphone amidst loud applause from hundreds of people who have read her book *Buddha's Sister*. She stands very still, opening herself to the mood of her audience. She feels warmth and admiration and a gentle undercurrent of lust. And she senses a powerful desire for absolution: a longing to hear her say, "It is never too late to begin anew."

Into the hushed silence, Ina whispers, "I was a whore again today."

Her audience gasps.

"I wanted to see my father and mother. I haven't seen them in twenty-five years. When I called them this morning to arrange a visit, my father kept saying one word over and over again: no. Then he hung up and I was a whore again. My spirit wanted to leave my body because it felt so dirty and cold. I wanted to snort cocaine and smoke pot and be numb to everything so I could allow some unthinking man to violate me. You might say I was having a flashback, but I wasn't merely remembering the past, I *was* a whore again."

She pauses, knowing she has frightened some of her listeners into resistance, knowing she has torn away scars on the hearts of others.

"Buddha was a whore," she says softly. "If you believe he had thousands and millions of incarnations, you must believe he was many times a whore. And for those who doubt reincarnation as a fact of existence, for whom the life of Buddha is a metaphor of spiritual evolution, then I suggest to you that we have all experienced the misery of self-loathing in one form or another."

She takes a deep breath and exhales, feeling embraced by a strong current of love.

"Buddha's method for ridding ourselves of this misery is to recognize self-loathing as an illusory construct of redundant thoughts, and to allow the feelings produced by these thoughts to play out as we meditate, so we may watch the illusion dissolve into nothingness."

She waits a moment before resuming her talk in a more conversational tone.

"I was recently in Tibet studying the techniques used by farmers there for cultivating vegetables at high altitudes, and for the first time in twenty-five years I was overcome by a desire to make contact with my parents. I dreamt about them every night and thought about them every day. In my dreams and thoughts they were incredibly kind to me — loving and affectionate."

She closes her eyes and sees the faces of her parents as she saw them in her dreams.

"On my last day in Tibet, I was privileged to visit a spiritual master I have admired for many years. We sat together on a low bench in the morning sun outside her house, and she served me a bowl of black tea flavored with dark honey made by wild bees. We did not speak aloud. She is clairvoyant. Everyone who meets her says the same thing: you can *feel* her listening to your thoughts.

"After we drank our tea, she took my bowl from me and set it inside hers. Then she put her arms around me and held me for a long time — for several hours. I wept for most of that time and lived again a thousand agonies, all of which dissolved in the unwavering strength of her love.

"Then she washed my feet and tickled my toes and served me another bowl of her strong black tea. And then she said in her beautiful broken English, 'Ina you my mother.'"

THE FREEDOM
OF RESTRAINT

Luxuriating on a big blue towel on the warm sand, feeling drowsy and content in the autumn sun, Sarah groans at the sound of a clanging triangle calling her to meditation.

Gentle waves lap the shore — the air scented with honeysuckle. She closes her journal, caps her pen, and kneels for a moment, gazing in wonder at the shining sea and the golden cliffs and the turquoise sky.

"This is where I want to be," she says to a pelican gliding by. "I think I'll stay. So what if I miss *one* session?"

She laughs and rolls up her towel. "Come on, old body." She steps into her sandals and leaves her nest in the dunes. "Back to work."

She strides along the trail through a forest of oak and coastal pines, pleased with herself for resisting the temptation of an afternoon on the beach. She is a youthful woman of forty-eight, though it is only recently that she has begun to feel young and strong again. Two long and rancorous marriages to men of simmering fury, and the death of her only child — Donna, sixteen — left her in a coma of depression for many years. But time and loving friends and a marvelous therapist helped her make the long climb into the light where Buddha greeted her, and she began her trek along the middle way.

When she comes to Lizard Creek — so named for the blue-bellies who sunbathe on the rocks there — she catches a whiff of what for thirty years was her favorite herb, her antidepressant, her painkiller, her solace and motive and captor. Overwhelmed with curiosity to see who among her fellow apprentices would dare break a cardinal rule of their order, she leaves the trail and hurries up the creekside footpath.

As the pungent smell of burning cannabis grows stronger, she forgets all about Buddha. "What's today?" she murmurs, her mind jumbled with memories. "It's been two years since I had any. One little hit won't hurt."

She rounds a bend and steps into a cloud of smoke — sweet and grassy and utterly intoxicating to her. She ascends the stone steps beside tumbling Sumedha Falls and arrives at the edge of the swimming hole — Jules's Pool.

What she beholds is so astonishing and horrifying to her, she freezes in terror and disbelief. He who has been her most important guide through the darkness of despair — her impeccable teacher — sits in full lotus position, engulfed in an effluvium of white smoke erupting from a black ceramic bowl heaped with fist-sized buds of glistening *Cannabis sativa*.

Sunk in deep meditation, her teacher appears to be an incarnation of the warrior Buddha — his soul encased in the heavily muscled body of a man who labors mightily in the fields by day, practices strenuous yoga by night, and never misses a minute of the five hours of daily meditation required of the monks of his order. Yet here he sits engulfed in clouds of a forbidden intoxicant — enemy of awareness — the very substance Sarah has worked so diligently to leave behind.

Unable to contain this seeming contradiction in her logical mind, Sarah cries, "Roshi! What are you doing?"

He opens his eyes and gazes at her without a trace of surprise. "Come sit with me," he says softly. "This is the very hour in which I said goodbye to this enchantment thirty years ago. Come. Come watch it burn with me."

"But I'll be late for meditation," she whispers, breathless with fear.

"No, no," he says, stirring the buds with a little stick. "We have a whole hour."

"But I heard the triangle," she says, her terror giving way to wonder.

"I rang it just for you," he says, offering her the stirring stick. "Happy birthday."

Community

Joe — a fearless man of seventy — clicks on the front porch light and unlocks the door, wondering who could be knocking so late on such a stormy night.

A pretty young woman — frightened — stands in the light with two small children, a boy six, a girl four. They are all soaking wet, the boy shivering. Joe has seen this woman and her children somewhere before but can't attach names to them.

"Come in," he says, opening the door wide. "Wow. What a storm."

The children hesitate, but their mother herds them in ahead of her, Joe stepping aside as they enter, the embers of the evening's fire shimmering in the hearth at the far end of the spacious living room.

Agnes — vivacious, tireless, sixty-eight — enters from the kitchen, peers over the top of her reading glasses at the bedraggled children, and says, "Let's get out of those wet clothes before we catch cold."

When the children — Kyle and Ashley — are fast asleep on the living room futon, their mother, Susan, sits with Joe and Agnes at the kitchen table and tells her story.

Pregnant and on her own at seventeen in a small town in Tennessee, she moved in with a willing older man — not the father of Kyle — who soon proved to be a vicious drunk. She ran away from him after seven months of his continuous abuse.

Three months later, in Nashville, fearing her baby boy would be taken away by the authorities, she married a smooth-talking alcoholic with whom she had Ashley, only to discover that her new mate was sexually abusing Kyle.

She fled again and spent two terrifying years raising her children in homeless shelters and abandoned buildings.

Exhausted and suicidal, she married a New Orleans policeman who seemed at first to be a knight in shining armor and turned out to be a sadistic psychopath. After being held prisoners for nine months in his fortress-like home, she pulled off an elaborate escape and hitchhiked with her children across America to California.

Since their arrival in the golden state, she and Kyle and Ashley have been sleeping in abandoned cars, gathering cans and bottles to redeem for cash, and going door-to-door offering to wash windows and pull weeds.

Susan and her children know Joe from a chance meeting at the community garden. They had gone there to look for clothes and food in the Free Box, and Joe was weeding and watering the three plots belonging to his household. He gave Susan a bag of zucchini and broccoli, and invited the children to help him harvest the hundreds of ripe cherry tomatoes, most of which he insisted they take with them.

"So a while later we were in this neighborhood picking up

cans and bottles," she explains, "and Kyle saw you come down your driveway on your bike, and he said, 'Hey, Mama that's the cherry tomato man,' so that's how we knew where you lived. So today when they towed our car away with all our stuff, and the storm hit, I didn't know what else to do, so…"

She bows her head and weeps. Agnes puts her arms around her and says, "Don't worry, dear. You're safe now."

At breakfast, Susan and Kyle and Ashley make the acquaintance of the two other adults — Seth and Marlene — who share the house with Joe and Agnes. They are a Buddhist household, members of a loose-knit community comprising a dozen homes in the vicinity and several others scattered across the country. The *sangha* convenes on Thursday evenings at the local Unitarian church for a dharma talk and meditation, and to keep everyone abreast of what's happening in the community.

Swamping his blueberry pancakes in maple syrup, Seth — a lanky man of sixty — says, "You know, I think there's a room open at Larue's house." He looks directly at Kyle. "You know who lives at Larue's house?"

"Who?" says Kyle, his mouth full of pancake.

"Danny," says Marlene — a big, round woman of forty-six. "He's been dying to live with people his own age."

"Is *he* six?" asks Ashley, eating with her fingers despite her mother's protestations. "Cuz Kyle's six and I'm four only I'm *almost* five."

"Nuh uh." Kyle glowers at her. "You *just* turned four."

"I believe Danny is five," says Seth, winking at Ashley. "Going on thirty-seven."

"I'll call Larue," says Agnes, resting her hands on Susan's shoulders. "See if we can come over and take a look at the room."

"Oh, no," says Susan, shaking her head. "You've done so much already. I'm just gonna get the kids cleaned up and we'll get out of here."

"Rained two inches last night," says Joe, coming in the back door with an armload of firewood. "Gonna rain all day. You want to help me start a fire, Kyle?"

"Yeah!" He jumps down from his chair. "I *love* fires."

"I wanna help, too," says Ashley, wiping her hands on her sweatshirt.

"No!" Kyle folds his arms and glares at the ground. "He asked *me*."

"I was hoping you'd help me make cookies," says Marlene, nodding hopefully at Ashley.

"I'll help you make cookies, too," says Kyle, following Joe into the living room. "After we get the fire going."

"There's plenty of work for everybody," says Joe, kneeling by the fireplace and dropping his load of wood. "No need to fight about it."

Kyle starts to cry. "But you asked *me*, not her."

"That's true," says Joe, feeling himself about to cry, too. "Thanks for pointing that out. My fault."

"Larue?" says Agnes, smiling into the phone. "Wonder if you could come over sometime today. I want you to meet a friend of ours. She and her two kids are looking for a room to rent. I just thought…" She listens. "*Two* rooms? Even better. Yeah, we're making rainy-day cookies. Come on by."

"I'm gonna miss my bus if I don't hurry," says Seth, gulping the last of his coffee. "Marlene, might I prevail upon you to wash my dishes? I will credit your karmic account accordingly."

"*I'll* do the dishes," says Susan, jumping up. "I'll clean the kitchen, wash the windows. Heck, I'll clean the whole house if you'll let me."

"*Let* you?" Seth bows to her. "If anybody tries to stop you, they'll have to deal with me."

Three days later at Larue's house, Danny, who is *going* to be six, shows Kyle and Ashley around the place and introduces them to the two cats, Felix and Mr. Boo, the three rats, Clyde, Lorna, and Ringo, the four nameless goldfish, and Herman, the enormous golden retriever.

Meanwhile, Susan sits on a big brown sofa in the living room trying to stay calm for this second official meeting with her prospective housemates. Larue is forty-seven, a big, relaxed woman, the single mother of Danny. Roger, forty-eight, is a rakishly handsome ballet dancer turned clothing designer, and Paul, fifty-seven, is a tall, slender man with long, snowy-white hair, a high school Drama teacher. Roger and Paul have been partners for nineteen years.

"Well, we've decided we'd like you to move in," says Larue, looking up from her knitting to smile at Susan. "A unanimous

Yes, and Danny voted twice."

"I know you know this," says Paul, somewhat sheepishly, "but we're a drug-free community and in this particular house there's no liquor allowed. Are you cool with that?"

"Absolutely." Susan looks anxiously at each of them. "But, um…you know I'm so grateful for everything you and Agnes and Joe and everybody has done for us, but…why are you doing this for me?"

Roger smiles. "It's what was done for each of us. It's how we all came to be here."

"What do you mean?" Susan opens her arms to receive Ashley sauntering in for a hug.

"It's why we're here," says Paul, pouring out the tea into four waiting cups. "It's the foundation of our community."

"The *sangha*?" says Susan, loving the sound of the word.

"The *sangha*," says Roger, handing around the steaming cups. "Buddha said the *sangha* was more important than any other single aspect of the Buddhist way of life."

"Each of us was alone in one way or another until we came into the community," says Larue, inhaling the scent of her tea before sipping. "Of course some people don't choose to stay. But I think you will."

"Why do you think that?" Susan steals a glance at Larue. "I mean, you hardly know me."

"I have great intuition." Larue smiles, savoring her tea. "And Joe and Agnes think you're marvelous, and they're pretty much infallible."

"Hey Mom," says Danny, running into the room a step ahead of Kyle. "Guess what?"

"What, honey?" says Larue, giving her boy a hug.

"Me and Kyle," he says, pausing dramatically, "are gonna be *best* friends."

"Kyle and I," says Larue, kissing his cheek.

"What about me?" asks Ashley, pouting at Danny.

"See?" says Kyle, nodding sagely. "I told you."

GOD

Joan and Margaret, best friends in high school and out of touch since, live on opposite sides of the world. Joan belongs to an esoteric sect of fundamentalist Christians; Margaret is an easy-going Buddhist. Joan lives with her husband, Phil, a plumber, and their seven children near Westphalia, Kansas. Margaret, a journalist and photographer, lives in Stuttgart, Germany, with her only child Anais.

At their thirtieth high school reunion in Belmont, California, Margaret won the Came Farthest To Attend award and Joan won Parent of the Youngest Child award — her seventh child born twenty years after her sixth.

"Not really an accident," said Joan as she accepted the award, rosy-cheeked in front of her applauding, laughing classmates, "but certainly a blessed surprise."

Joan and Margaret were drawn to each other after thirty years apart just as they were drawn to each other in high school. None of their external differences could hold a candle to the warmth they felt inside when they were with each other.

They exchanged addresses, wrote frequently, and now — two years after their reunion — Joan and her daughter, Paula, are spending a week in Barcelona with Margaret and Anais. Joan and Margaret have both just turned fifty. Anais is eighteen, Paula twenty-two.

Anais, her father Algerian, is a brown-skinned beauty with startling green eyes and curly black hair. She is fluent in five languages and conversant in three others. According to her mother, "Anais was born a full-blown adult."

Paula is a big-boned blond with pale blue eyes, voluptuous lips, and a lifelong tendency to daydream. She is soon to be married to a hog farmer chosen for her by the elders of their tiny congregation. She expressed no interest in accompanying her mother to Spain, and only agreed to make the trip after her father commanded her to go.

On their third day in Barcelona, Margaret and Joan leave their suite an hour before dawn to take pictures of the waking city. Anais, having stayed out late at a dance club, rises at nine, showers, and is on her way out the door as Paula emerges from the bathroom.

"Um," says Paula, waving to Anais as if from a great distance, "are you going for coffee?"

Anais nods, hoping her dour expression will dissuade Paula from coming with her.

"Um...could I tag along?"

"If you want," says Anais, forcing a smile. "Or I could bring something back for you."

"I'd like to get out," says Paula, her tone beseeching. "I'll be ready in a second."

In a café with high ceilings and colorful abstract paintings on brick walls, Anais orders their omelets and coffee drinks in flawless Spanish, then banters in rapid-fire French with an amorous young man from Mali.

Anais tells Paula in unadorned California English, "He says he's got a friend for you, too."

"Not me," says Paula, glancing up from a fashion magazine. "I'm engaged."

Anais lights a cigarette and opens her notebook to draw a picture of Paula. Anais has been sketching people and writing about them since she was five years old. What began as an imitation of her mother's work has become the foundation of her budding career as an artist and writer.

"Can I have one?" asks Paula, nodding wide-eyed at Anais's cigarette. "Might be my last chance before I get married."

Anais gives her cigarette to Paula and lights another for herself. Paula blushes as she takes her first puff, never having experienced such casual intimacy with anyone.

"I took Spanish for a year in high school," says Paula, shaking her head. "But I only remember *quiero* and *gracias*."

"That's all you need," says Anais, warming to Paula for the first time. "*I want* and *thank you*."

"You rattle it off like you were born here." Paula laughs self-consciously. "Heck, I have trouble with English."

"You'd be fluent in a month if you lived here," says Anais, beginning her sketch. "You have fabulous eyes and a very sexy mouth."

"Who?" says Paula, shocked. "Me?"

"Sí señorita." Anais smiles at the nascent drawing. "Muy bonita."

"Yes, girl, very pretty," says Paula, looking up at the ceiling and nodding. "I guess I know more words than I thought."

"May I ask you something?" says Anais, glancing back and forth from Paula to the page of her notebook — rapid strokes coalescing into a pleasing likeness of a lovely young woman just opening her eyes to the world.

"Sure, if I can ask *you* something." Paula smiles shyly at their handsome waiter as he places the latte — a big green bowl brimming with steamed milk — before her.

"Un doble," he murmurs, searching her eyes with his.

"Gracias," says Paula, breathless in her first exchange with a Spaniard.

He nods ever so slightly to acknowledge Paula's thanks and places a double espresso — dense black coffee in a miniature white cup on a red saucer — in front of Anais.

"Puedo ver?" he asks softly.

Anais nods, keeping her focus on Paula and the emerging image.

He steps around behind her and gazes down at her drawing. "De veras." He looks from the drawing to Paula. "De veras."

"What's that mean?" asks Paula, watching him walk away.

"It's true." Anais nods. "Or…it's truthful."

"Um…Anais?"

"What?"

"How come they gave me a bowl?" She frowns at her latte. "You think maybe they ran out of mugs?"

"That's how they serve lattes here." She adds a few strokes to the sturdy chin. "So, do you *want* to get married?"

"Of course." Paula drops her voice to a whisper. "It's what God made me for. To, you know, be a helpmate to my husband and bear his children."

Anais stops drawing. "You really believe that?"

"Never believed anything else." Paula shrugs. "You think it's stupid?"

"No," says Anais, resuming her sketching. "I'd like to get married and be a help to my husband. I don't know if I want to have children, but I'd like to be married someday."

The omelets arrive. They each make silent prayers over their food before eating.

"So, what I wanted to ask you," says Paula, waving to their waiter, "is about Buddhism. You and your mom are Buddhists, right?"

"De veras," says Anais, curious to hear what Paula wants from their waiter.

"Sí señorita?" asks the handsome man, his gaze lingering on Paula's lips. "Que se quiere?"

"Could I get a mug for this?" She taps her latte bowl. "I can't get a good grip."

"Pichel," says Anais, translating. "Ella no puede agarrar el tazón."

"Gracias." Paula nods enthusiastically as the waiter carries her latte away.

"So what do you want to know about Buddhism?" asks Anais, resuming her drawing of Paula.

"Do you, like, believe in God?" asks Paula, her pronunciation of *God* imbued with reverence.

"In a way." Anais adds the last few lines to Paula's face. "Only I don't believe God is some huge all-powerful *guy* living in some heavenly kingdom in the sky."

"Well, then, what do you believe he is?" asks Paula, her eyes fixed on the approaching mug in the beautiful hands of their handsome waiter.

"I believe God is everything there's ever been and everything that is and everything that ever will be." Anais holds out her notebook to Paula. "The essential ground of being."

"Wow," says Paula, awestruck by her portrait. "This is amazing, Anais. It's incredible. I look so...I don't know. Pretty?"

"You're beautiful," says Anais, tapping her tiny cup to indicate she wants another espresso.

Their waiter stands behind Paula looking at the portrait of her, his voice sweet music in her ears — two words repeated. "De veras. De veras."

CRAVING

Lewis is madly in love with Anita and painfully bewildered by her attitude toward him. She seems to delight in his company, and they never part without her insisting they get together again, and soon! But if he embraces her in greeting or at parting, she becomes a manikin in his arms.

After months of anguishing about her, Lewis invites Anita to tea with the intention of declaring his love and confusion. She arrives looking especially lovely, and launches into the latest news about her mother in France, her brother in Manitoba, and her friends scattered hither and yon. Sipping strong black tea in his sunny kitchen, she goes on and on about her son and how successful he is after many years of difficulty.

As Lewis waits for an opportunity to express his feelings for Anita, he realizes that their conversations are always this one-sided, that he has, in fact, hallucinated a relationship with her.

Completing her effusive accolades of her son, Anita gazes at Lewis with what he has heretofore assumed to be the look of love, but which he now understands is a brief and perfunctory seduction of his lonely psyche. "And how are *you*?" she asks, her voice warm and husky and sounding as if they are only a few moments away from making love.

This question from her, he now understands, is the crux of their involvement and the source of his bafflement. That she asks him about himself in such a seemingly intimate way has been sufficient over and over again to ignite his craving for intimacy. And since these words of concern for him come from the lovely mouth of her lovely face attached to her lovely body, it is she he wishes to love.

He also knows — and this, too, he admits to himself for the first time — that if his answer to her question should be longer than a sentence or two, or if he dares hint that his emotional state has something to do with her, she will signify her displeasure by a fluttering of her eyelids and a barely perceivable grimace pursuant to a glance at her watch, followed by a lengthy explanation of why she can't stay and what the rest of her day holds for her. And then, of course, will come her protestation — amplified by a delicious smile — that they **must** see each other again, and soon!

"I'm fine," he answers quietly. "More tea?"

She glances at her watch. "Oh, God. Look at the time."

He checks the clock above his stove. She has been with him exactly fifty minutes — the length of time he spends with his psychotherapist.

"And I finally *got*," he says to his therapist, speaking of Anita, "that I was endowing her with every characteristic I ever hoped for in a mate, though I don't think she possesses a single one of them."

A silence falls, his therapist a man of few words.

"Well," Lewis continues, "she *is* beautiful, and her voice…"

His therapist watches with compassion as Lewis begins to weep.

"Her voice," Lewis murmurs, seeing Anita's tender lips, "went straight to my heart."

Loving-kindness

Mr. Maloney is complaining about the coffee being burnt, which it most definitely is not. A man and a woman in a corner booth are saying vicious things to each other. A tearful child is begging to be held by a woman who would rather growl into a mobile phone.

Susan fills Mr. Maloney's cup with fresh coffee, piping hot. He glowers at her. "This is burnt, too. Can't you smell it?"

"No, Mr. Maloney, I can't," says Susan, a hard edge to her voice. "I just brewed this pot."

"Then the beans are bad," he says, calling after her as she moves out from behind the counter to refresh the myriad cups.

Tania, the other breakfast waitress, her arms laden with empty dishes, hurries past Susan and murmurs, "The guys at table seven scrammed without paying their bill."

"Oh, no," Susan groans, rushing to the big table by the window in the vain hope of finding money hidden in the wreckage of four enormous breakfasts — steaks, waffles, omelets, fresh-squeezed orange juice, and two rounds of fancy coffee drinks — a hundred-dollar tab.

"Hey, lady," barks a bleary-eyed woman at the next table. "Can a person get some service here?"

Susan fills the woman's coffee cup and takes her order, apologizing for the wait.

"Lousy management." The woman sneers at Susan. "You people think you can just slop together…"

Susan turns away.

"Hey, I'm in the middle of a sentence," says the woman. "You rude bitch."

Susan wheels back around. "Don't you call me that. If you can't be civil, get out."

"But I was talking to you," says the woman, her eyes filling with tears. "I was in the middle of a sentence."

"You were in the middle of insulting me." Susan keeps her voice low. "We're very busy. Okay? We're doing the best we can."

The door swings open and a cool breeze precedes Alana and Isaac — she a tall woman of eighty-five, he her portly companion of fifty. They bow to Susan. She nods emphatically, which means their customary booth is ready.

Several minutes pass before Susan is free to attend to Alana and Isaac. As she approaches their booth, they open their eyes at the conclusion of their silent prayers — their faces creased with smiles. Susan sets a shiny blue teapot brimming with just-boiled water in front of Isaac. He nods gratefully.

Alana touches Susan's hand. "We've brought a delicious oolong along this morning. You *must* try some."

"Oolong along," says Isaac, shaking a goodly number of dark green pellets — tightly rolled tea leaves — into the pot. "I like the sound of that. Oolong along. Along along oolong."

Susan laughs. "You two are a breath of fresh air, let me tell you."

"Oh, please tell us," says Alana, laughing with her. "We love it."

"It's why we come here." Isaac surveys the crowded café. "And to be with all these fabulous people."

"The usual?" asks Susan, no longer feeling so overwhelmed and hopeless.

"Yes, dear." Alana touches Susan's hand again. "And do tell Chaco he's a genius."

"A magus," says Isaac, lifting the lid of the teapot to watch the leaves unfurl. "And when you have a moment, I'd love a colossal glass of orange juice."

Susan turns away from them, a sweet smile on her face. She sees that all the other customers are content for the moment — Tania plying the room with a full pot of coffee — so she steps into the kitchen where Chaco, the imperturbable chef, is enjoying a brief respite from the grill, the smoke from his freshly lit cigar borne away by the powerful fan.

"Alana and Isaac," she says to him, sitting down to rest her legs for a moment. "The usual. And they send their compliments in advance."

"Thank God for them." He stubs out his stogie and washes his hands. "The usual."

Susan pushes off from her chair and returns to the fray, Mr. Maloney beckoning to her.

"Yes, dear?" she asks, smiling down on him. "What can I get you?"

"Any apple pie left?" he asks, his tone conciliatory.

"One last piece," she says, gazing over his head at the little girl snuggled in her mother's arms, the angry couple holding hands, the bleary-eyed woman laughing with Tania, and Alana and Isaac reverently sipping their tea. "Just for you."

Happiness

Gerald is turning the soil in the narrow bed of earth that runs the length of the south-facing side of the old house he rents — October more than half over. He intends to plant snow peas where the sun and white walls conspire to keep the ground relatively warm throughout the winter months.

He is not conscious that it has been seven years to the day since he learned of his wife's unfaithfulness to him for all of their eighteen years of marriage. He is divorced now and has grown accustomed to living alone. The discovery of his wife's secret life shattered his confidence in himself and in his closest friends — two of them being his wife's lovers. He sold his law practice after finalizing the divorce and has been unemployed ever since.

His days are spent reading, taking long walks, listening to music, writing letters to friends, and sitting still. His money is nearly gone. He has no intention of practicing law again, though he has yet to decide how he will earn his living.

His shovel sinks into the dry ground, and as he turns the soil, it crumbles into tiny fragments, leaving only the smallest of clods. Six years ago the soil here was dense clay, but hundreds of buckets of kitchen compost and the labor of ten thousand worms have made the soil rich and pliable.

Recalling how difficult this task was a few years ago, Gerald smiles at the ease with which he now readies the bed. He rakes the ground until it is essentially level, and creates a little dam at the slightly downhill end of the bed. Now he kneels and, using his index finger, draws an inch-deep channel in the dirt some ten inches out from the wall of the house.

He reaches into his pocket and brings forth a packet of snow pea seeds. The planting instructions promise bushes thirty inches tall—self-supporting. But Gerald knows the vines will be much taller than thirty inches and will require support to keep from sprawling. He wonders why the seed sellers boast that the bushes will stand on their own when they never do, and he smiles again, happy to know the gangly plants will need his bamboo poles and string.

He drops the pale green pearls into the rough channel—one pearl every three or four inches along the way—and covers them with the rich soil. Now he stands and treads on the row, pressing the dirt down upon the seeds.

The bright blue hose is nearby, the water running noiselessly onto rust red chrysanthemums—wild children of a housewarming gift from a thoughtful friend.

As he takes up the hose from the mums—survivors of a dry summer and his occasional neglect—he remembers his wife and the sorrow of their parting. Now he presses his thumb into the mouth of the hose and sprays the water onto the new bed of peas — the grayish soil turning black—and he remembers his wife's ecstatic face as they mated on sun-dappled sheets.

The bed becomes a pool with spray dappling the surface — a rainbow appearing in the mist near Gerald's hand.

HUMILITY

Thomas is seventy-seven. His wife, Denise, died unexpectedly in her sleep a year and a month ago.

Thomas's work — the completion of the seventh and final volume of an exhaustive history of the English language — has not progressed a word since Denise's death. An oppressive sorrow has lain upon Thomas for these thirteen months, and he has little hope of living beyond his grief.

A tall, lean Englishman with pale blue eyes and red hair going gray, Thomas is roused from his stupor at the kitchen table — his bagel and tea untouched — by loud rapping on the front door. His first thought is to ignore the summons, but the rapping persists, so he reluctantly rises and goes to the door.

"Yes?" he says, frowning curiously at an enormous young man with dark brown skin, a shaved head, and muscular arms covered with tattoos.

"I'm Oz," says the young man, holding out a piece of paper to Thomas. "You the tutor?"

"I don't believe so." Thomas peers at the paper and realizes through a fog of despair that his daughter, Maureen, must have gone ahead and fulfilled her threat to sign him up for after-school duty.

"Got the address right," says Oz, his voice deep and sonorous. "Seven seven six."

"I stand corrected." Thomas chuckles at his daughter's audacity. "Come in."

"Like a library," says Oz, stopping on the threshold to gaze around the living room, every inch of wall given over to bookshelves. "You read all these books?"

"Most of them more than once." Thomas scans the thousands of volumes for any he might have skipped.

"Smells old in here." Oz wrinkles his nose. "You got a sunny room?"

"The kitchen," says Thomas, leading the way. "I'll make a fresh pot of green tea."

"I ain't never had no green tea," says Oz, pausing in the hallway to look at a picture of Thomas as a young Oxford scholar. "Get a buzz?"

"There is some caffeine in green tea," Thomas replies, gesturing to the kitchen table. "Make yourself at home."

"Coffee jitters me bad," says Oz, taking a seat from which he can observe Thomas. "Green tea don't do that, do it?"

"No, it's more subtle." Thomas fills the kettle. "It invigorates in a wholly different way than coffee."

"You show more accent than your daughter," says Oz, nodding his approval of the cheerful room. "Me likes."

"Oh, so you do know my daughter." Thomas sets the kettle atop the flame. "That was my supposition."

"Word," says Oz, grinning at Thomas. "She chose me special just for you."

"Why is that, do you suppose?" Thomas peruses his collection of teas and decides on a pungent green from Taiwan.

"She flunked me twice." Oz nods slowly. "But she knows I'm not stupid."

"No, you're obviously exceedingly intelligent." Thomas clears away his lunch dishes. "May I offer you something to eat?"

"No." Oz looks glumly at the floor and cracks his knuckles. "How come you use that word? Exceedingly? Means more than enough, yeah? Like you think I'm *very* smart. Which I am, but…how come you think so?"

"The way you take things in." Thomas sits down opposite Oz. "The way you listen and respond. We've been in real conversation from our very first moment together, and that's quite rare in my experience."

Oz nods. "You write books?"

"I have written books," says Thomas, studying Oz's handsome face, the chiseled cheeks and jaw, "though I doubt I will ever write another."

"How come?" asks Oz, hearing sorrow in Thomas's voice. "Must be nice to write a good book."

"I have lost my inspiration," says Thomas, thinking of Denise and how everything he wrote, he wrote for her. "I'm old now. Tired."

"So why you want to be a tutor?" Oz rises to quiet the whistling kettle.

Thomas is about to reply that he *doesn't* want to be a tutor, that this is all his daughter's doing, that he's very sorry but he's just not up to it. Instead, after a thoughtful pause, he says,

"Perhaps I can still be useful to someone."

"Someone maybe like me," says Oz, shaking dry tea leaves into his hand to inspect them. "You wanna show me how to make this drink?"

"Ah," says Thomas, raising a knowing finger. "The art of tea."

FEAR

Tolman — forty-eight — is seven feet tall, his shoulders so broad he has to turn sideways to pass through most doorways. His skin is the color of dark honey, his black hair lustrous and curly — his antecedents Moroccan and Russian. He is the sole employee of Estelle Fuller, a renowned garden designer who declines to use any motorized tools in her work. Tolman has been her motor, as it were, for nine years, and there is nothing in the way of making a garden he cannot accomplish with his fantastic strength and keen understanding of soil and rocks and trees.

Estelle — fifty-seven — is five feet tall and weighs one hundred pounds. A professional dancer before becoming a designer of gardens, her white skin is quick to freckle in the sun and her short red hair is laced with gray. When she stands beside Tolman, perusing some aspect of a garden's installation, she appears to be less than half his size, which is not an illusion.

When it comes to making gardens together, they seem possessed of a single mind — communication between them clairvoyant — and they speak aloud for pleasure rather than from necessity. Yet for all their intimacy in the making of gardens, their lives away from work rarely intersect — each having entirely erroneous ideas about how the other lives.

Tolman believes Estelle has a lover, a busy social life, and frequent contact with her daughter and son. Estelle believes Tolman has legions of female admirers and a wide circle of friends and fellow musicians. Yet both are shy and single and essentially reclusive — and both long to be otherwise.

The truth is, they are passionately in love with each other, yet neither believes the other could possibly feel this way. Tolman fears Estelle finds him too big and too quiet and too unremarkable, while Estelle fears Tolman finds her too small and too old and too intellectual.

Estelle's custom is to devote December and January to pursuits other than gardening — persistent rain rendering outdoor work unfeasible. Aside from the few days around Christmas when her children come to visit, she spends most of her time reading, writing, and designing the rough forms of gardens she and Tolman will create together in the spring.

Tolman traditionally spends those two winter months at a friend's farm in Baja California. When he is not writing songs or working on the farm, he takes long treks into the mountains and to remote beaches on the Sea of Cortez.

On the last day of a stormy November, Estelle and Tolman are putting the finishing touches on a garden surrounding a large pond nestled among seven dramatic outcroppings of granite. Twenty Japanese maples line a gravel path circumnavigating the pool in which lilies and koi will abound. A copse of enormous ferns dominates the shady eastern flank of the garden, and each outcropping of granite is partnered with a gangly cherry tree destined for graceful maturity.

As they clean their tools and prepare to go their separate ways, Estelle wants to jump up on a big rock, look Tolman in the eye and say, "I *really* want to spend time with you over the holidays." And Tolman wants to say, "Come to Baja with me."

But Estelle only manages to say, "So…I'll see you tomorrow. Our last day until February."

And Tolman, having rehearsed his invitation to her a hundred times, only musters a quiet, "Yes. Tomorrow."

Estelle has written — but never sent — countless letters to Tolman — each a passionate elucidation of how wonderful she thinks he is and how very much she would like to explore the possibility of becoming his lover. He, in turn, has written dozens of love songs for Estelle, but has never had the nerve to sing them to her.

On the evening before their last day together, Estelle sits on her living room sofa — her cat, Fiona, curled up beside her — and writes yet another loving confession to Tolman, while in a pub two miles away Tolman sits sipping ale and jotting down lyrics to a ballad in which every other line rhymes with *Estelle*.

Rising from her armchair to place a big log on the dwindling fire, Estelle smiles to think how easily Tolman could lift this log with one hand, while she must use both hands and all her strength to lower it onto the embers.

Watching the flames spring up around the log, Estelle recalls the precise moment Tolman cut this piece of wood for her — the oak yielding to his huge buck saw like a loaf of bread opening to a sharp knife. And thinking of his astonishing strength, she realizes that what she fears more than anything is a failed love affair with Tolman that would ruin their friendship and make it impossible to continue working together.

"I can't imagine making gardens with anyone but him," she says to the fire. "I only want to do it with Tolman."

Meanwhile, Tolman rides his bicycle through a cold drizzle to the marina, steps aboard the dysfunctional sailboat he calls home, and descends into the galley where he must kneel to avoid bumping his head on the ceiling.

He crawls to his bed and lies on his back, gazing up at moonlit clouds — his skylight leaking — and sighs mightily as the wharf cats, Tom and Boy, find their places atop the vast expanse of Tolman's torso.

Petting the cats, he recites a timeworn litany of despair. "I'm too big for her. I scare her. I'm not sophisticated enough for her. She's wealthy and owns a fabulous house. I own a guitar. She's written books. She's famous. I'm nobody. I…"

He stops himself, gently sheds the cats, and crawls to his stove to put a kettle on for tea.

"I'm moving," he says, surprising himself with the proclamation. "I'm tired of crawling around in my kitchen."

The sun comes out for the last day Estelle and Tolman will work together until spring.

Estelle sits on a boulder across the pond from Tolman, watching him adjust the position of a seven hundred pound cube of granite occupying the center shelf of the seven-foot-high waterfall. Tolman is naked to the waist — cold water tumbling over him as he strains to move the massive stone.

"There," says Estelle, dazzled by the heroic sight of Tolman cloaked in roiling water. "Try it there."

Tolman steps away from the waterfall — a thick gush of water dropping unimpeded for three feet before striking the granite cube and exploding into frothy spray.

"Not bad," says Estelle, her eyes drawn more to Tolman than to the waterfall. "A bit bombastic, but maybe we need that. This garden is so peaceful. What do you think?"

"I have an idea," he says, nodding humbly. "May I?"

"Of course," she says, longing to join him in the water.

He wraps his arms around the massive cube and pulls it forward so the water now falls *behind* the stone before rising up and flowing over as a glassy scrim that penetrates deep into the pool — murmuring musically.

"Yes!" cries Estelle, her heart pounding. "Yes, Tolman. Just what I want."

He turns to her and says in harmony with the singing falls, "Just what I want, too, Estelle."

Skillful Speech

The ringing phone becomes the finale of Don's dream. He opens his eyes, surprised to find it still so dark. He knocks his glasses off the nightstand as he reaches for the phone.

"Yes?" he mumbles, his voice thick with sleep.

"You were *sleeping*?" asks a high-pitched voice. "How can you possibly sleep through this?"

"Jerome? What are you talking about?"

"The dogs!" cries Jerome. "The fucking dogs. They've been howling for hours."

"What time is it?"

"Almost five," says Jerome, disgusted. "We've been up since three."

"I'm sorry, Jer…"

"How can you not *hear* them? You told me you were a light sleeper."

"Which dogs are we talking about?"

"Are you serious?" asks Jerome, his rage palpable. "They're right behind your house."

"My bedroom is at the front and I have my bedroom door closed, so…"

"But you *must* be able to hear them now. Jesus, Don. Are you deaf? They sound like rampaging elephants."

"I'll go see," says Don, speaking softly.

131

"I'm coming over," says Jerome, hanging up.

Don opens his bedroom door and hears the plaintive whimpering of a spaniel and the anguished howling of a wolfhound. He wanders through his kitchen to the sliding glass door where Jerome is standing with clenched fists — the cries of the miserable dogs resounding in the morning air.

"Here's the number for Animal Control." Jerome thrusts a piece of paper at Don. "*And* the assholes' phone number. They have their answering machine on, but leave a message anyway. I know they're there. They're just afraid to talk to me."

"I will leave them a message," says Don, reacting to an upsurge of howling. "This is inexcusable."

"I could kill them." Jerome grits his teeth and shakes his head. "I haven't had a good night's sleep in a week."

Don does not call Animal Control, but he does write a letter that he slips under the front door of the house belonging to the owners of the bellowing dogs.

My dear neighbors,
We think you must be unaware of the volume and
persistency of the howling, whimpering, and whining
that emanate from your backyard at all hours of the day
and night. We are sure that if you were aware of how
intrusive and disheartening this cacophony is to your
neighbors, you would do something to mitigate these
symptoms of your dogs' suffering.

We wonder why your dogs are so unhappy. We invite you to come to our back door and experience our difficulty in carrying on a happy, productive life in the midst of such heartrending yowling. We are absolutely certain you want to do what's best for them and your community.

Many Thanks,
*   Your backyard neighbors*

Don is sitting at the kitchen table the next morning, sipping tea and writing a postcard to a friend, when Jerome bounds up the back steps with a jubilant smile on his face.

"We did it!" he cries. "Not a howl or a whimper all night." He smacks his fist into his palm. "Nothing like a visit from the men in blue to strike fear into the hearts of cowards."

"You called the police?" asks Don, frowning in surprise.

"Well, Animal Control," says Jerome, nodding emphatically. "I assume they came out right after you called. They said they'd only come if they got multiple complaints."

"Ah," says Don, sipping his tea. "And who else did you get to call them?"

"Just you and me," says Jerome, grinning triumphantly. "That's all it took."

RIGHT LIVELIHOOD

Haron sits on a wooden bench awaiting his train. A bashful man, forty-seven, with a boyish face and short gray hair, Haron has never been in a relationship with a woman — not counting his mother — that lasted more than six months. The women he is attracted to — women his own age or somewhat older than he — always seem to find him lacking, whereas women much younger than he seem to find him irresistible.

Haron's most recent relationship — the one that lasted six months — was with a woman half his age, and though she adored him and wanted to marry him, and though he admired her wit and sensuality and emotional honesty, he was never comfortable with the idea of such a young beauty loving such an elderly pauper as he perceives himself to be.

He has seventeen minutes to wait, so he decides to finish the drawing he began this morning at the breakfast table. He makes his drawings in a large notebook using a fine-tipped pen and black ink. His drawings are of whatever he sees directly in front of him — whimsical, poignant, mysterious renderings of the placement of objects in space — tableaus imbued with the promise of imminent change.

For reasons Haron has never fully understood, nearly everyone who sees his drawings wishes to possess them, and his lifetime habit — since he was three years old — is to give the finished drawing to whomever asks for it first. More often than not, the person sitting or standing beside Haron at the moment the picture is completed becomes its owner.

Over the years, many people have urged Haron to sell his art, but he secretly believes that if he ever takes money for his drawings, he will lose his ability to draw. And since drawing has been the one constant pleasure of his life, he has never been willing to risk the loss.

Yet lately he has been thinking seriously about trying to support himself by selling his drawings. Until two weeks ago, Haron was a clerk in an independent stationery store. But when the store was swallowed by a gargantuan corporation responsible for denuding one of the last ancient forests on earth — and despite grave uncertainty about what his next employment might be — Haron quit his job.

Prior to working in the stationery store he was a sandwich maker, a bicycle messenger, a gardener, a night watchman, and a toll taker on the Golden Gate Bridge, but he has no desire to retrace any of those steps. His rent is low, his needs are few, and he would love nothing better than to make ends meet by making art.

But what if he takes money for his art, and the unseen powers of the universe punish him by drying up the astonishing fluidity with which he renders the scenes of life? This is the question that plagues him now, and only ceases to bother him when he is lost in the magic of making a picture.

He is, as it happens, on his way to discuss this very dilemma with a therapist he met one evening some months ago in a pub. He was finishing a drawing of two men playing darts — the foreground filled with the looming presence of a pint glass brimming with dark ale — when the therapist, making her way through the crowded tavern, caught sight of the drawing, asked if she might buy it, and was pleasantly stunned when Haron simply removed the gorgeous thing from his notebook, placed it in one of the heavy cardboard envelopes he carries for just such purposes, and gave it to her. She insisted he take her card and call her if he ever needed the services of a therapist — or if he wanted to go out with her.

Her card — *Uma Ishkar, Motivational Psychotherapy* — now resides on Haron's refrigerator between the Van Gogh sunflower magnet and a Picasso Blue Period harlequin postcard, and never fails to remind him of the woman it represents — pretty and vivacious, her dark hair peppered with gray, her speech complex yet precise, her voice deep and full of confidence, her laughter infectious.

Uma was at the pub with a woman friend, but Haron is certain she is an unattached heterosexual. He has been afraid to call her because his previous experiences with women his own age or somewhat older than he have always ended sadly.

But so haunted is he by this question of taking money for his art, that he was emboldened to call Uma. When he explained who he was, she crowed with delight and went on and on about how much she loved his drawing — how studying the image had literally changed the way she looked at things.

However, when Haron said he wanted to make an appointment for therapy, the excitement in Uma's voice diminished dramatically.

A few minutes before his train is due, the station fills with commuters. A handsome woman — tall and blond and tan — wearing an elegant business suit and sensible shoes sits beside Haron, glances at his drawing and exclaims, "Oh my. That's fantastic. Is that your cat?"

"It is," says Haron, adding the last few strokes to the picture of Moby, a blotched tabby, sitting atop the morning newspaper, Haron's cup of tea in the foreground, the scene illuminated by slanting sunlight — the cat and newspaper and teacup casting marvelously curving shadows.

"I'm sure you must have a gallery representing you," says the woman, her eyes wide with interest, "but do you ever sell your work directly?"

"Well," says Haron, taking a deep breath, "if you'd like to buy this one, I'd be happy to sell it to you."

"Really?" says the woman, stunned by his reply. "What are you asking?"

Gazing at his drawing, Haron finds himself attached to his creation in a way he has never felt attached to anything he has ever made.

"How does…seven hundred dollars sound?"

"Oh, but that's giving it away," she says, gaping at him.

"Well, I've always given my drawings away." He smiles at

her. "I'm so glad you like it."

"Like it? I love it. Will you take a check?"

"I will," he says, carefully removing the page from his note-book. "And I'll put the drawing in a sturdy envelope so it won't get damaged in transit."

"I'll take it straight to my framer." She makes the check out for nine hundred. "And I *must* get on your mailing list so I don't miss your next show. Do you work large?"

"I may," says Haron, taking her check and her business card and sequestering them in his otherwise empty wallet. "Soon."

Just before his train arrives, Haron goes to the pay phone and calls Uma Ishkar, motivational psychotherapist, and asks if she would consider changing his therapy session to a dinner date — since he just sold a picture.

And Uma is positively overjoyed to say, "Yes!"

STATUES

"You know, of course," says Reginald, gazing out the kitchen window at the sitting Buddha beside the little pond in Kristen's garden, "statues of the Buddha are the antitheses of the fundamental teachings of Buddha."

"Nonsense." Kristen half-smiles and half-frowns at her old friend. "Nowhere is it written that Buddha was anti-statue."

"It is certainly *implied*." Reginald scowls imperiously as torrential rain batters the house. "Concretizing the metaphor is a cognitive attachment to illusion."

Kristen and Reginald are members of a small circle of highly intellectual Buddhists. She is sixty, he is fifty-nine — she a widow, he twice divorced. They are friends not lovers.

"I don't agree." Kristen lifts the lid of her teapot to assess the scent of the steeping oolong. "Needs another minute."

"As a matter of historical *fact*," Reginald continues disdainfully, "there were no statues of Buddha until several generations after his death." He clears his throat to foreshadow the importance of his next proclamation. "His original adherents, it is quite apparent, knew better than those lesser minds who came after."

"Pish tosh," says Kristen, pouring their tea. "I find statues of Buddha encouraging and thought provoking."

"You would." Reginald rolls his eyes. "You're stuck in a concept of form. Spaciousness versus emptiness."

"*Versus*?" She reddens. "So *you* must be stuck in polemics."

He scowls. "Just imagine your garden without that chunk of cement littering your ferns. Or is it too frighteningly natural without your bits of manufactured junk?"

"Imagine practice without ideas," she retorts, her head throbbing. "Imagine your mind free of dogma. Imagine no judgment."

"That statue is your ego." He smirks complacently. "You're just afraid of your non-self."

She sighs. "I wish you wouldn't resort to attacking *me*. I don't mind if you disagree with my ideas, but when you…"

"But we *are* ideas," he proclaims with a shout. "We are tangles of competing thought constructs vying for supremacy."

"And our souls?" Kristen's enormous gray tabby, Elvis, jumps onto her lap and butts his head against her breasts. "Are *they* thought constructs?"

"The idea of the soul is a very *minor* thought form." Reginald waves dismissively. "A mental statue, if you will. An idealized form. A wish fulfillment. An impediment to the experience of our innate emptiness, of our *being* emptiness."

"This body," she muses, weary of their conversation, "is a temporary coagulation of molecules meant for nothing, and only accidentally capable of self-replication?"

"Something like." He gulps down his tea. "Shall we go? Movie starts in fifteen minutes."

"Think I'll pass." She fakes a majestic yawn. "Feeling suddenly exhausted and hopeless."

"Mad at me?" He grins triumphantly. "Nothing personal. I just happen to believe that statues are infantile, primitive obfuscations of the higher realms of thought."

She nods. "Nothing personal."

The storm abates in the late afternoon. Kristen and Elvis go out to inspect the garden and breathe the rain-washed air. While her cat has a drink from the pond, Kristen stands before the gray stone statue of the placid, closed-eyed Buddha.

"I love your form," she says to him. "You inspire me to sit up straight and to seek balance. And to be patient."

A red leaf from the overhanging Japanese maple tumbles down and lands on the statue where the fingertips of the right hand touch the fingertips of the left and are held against the stomach at the navel.

Kristen — connected to everything — witnesses this reply.

GETTING WELL

Feeling happier than she's felt in a very long time, Dorothy, a robust woman of fifty-four, sits at her kitchen table savoring a mellow Dragonwell tea and delighting in an Edith Wharton short story about a brave divorcee.

The phone rings.

"Hello?" she says, chuckling at how strongly she identifies with the story's heroine.

"Don't *you* sound happy." It's Derek, Dorothy's ex-husband.

She tenses as she always does when she hears his voice, though she's been legally divorced from him for three years. "What's up?" she asks, dropping into the casual tone she uses when speaking to him now.

"I know this is going to sound funny," he begins, "but I've met a guy I think would be perfect for you, and you would be perfect for him."

"You're right," she says, fighting her impulse to hang up. "It does sound funny. I don't think…"

"A neighbor of yours," he continues. "Lives two blocks away. Let me give you his number."

"Why are you doing this?" Her stomach ties itself into the familiar knots of her previous life with him.

"I *knew* you'd say that," he complains, offended. "I'm doing this to help you, Dorothy. I met him at *your* favorite tennis courts. Jerry didn't show up, so Morgan and I hit a few. That's his name. Morgan. Great guy. Our age. Into lots of the same things you're into. So I just keep seeing you two together. I can't help it." He pauses. "Are you involved with somebody?"

"Is that what this is about? I thought we'd agreed…"

"No, no. I just don't understand why you don't want to give him a call."

"Did I *say* that?" she snaps, clenching her teeth as of old. "No, I didn't. I said…"

Two hours later, walking to a neighborhood café to meet her friend Lisa, Dorothy passes a handsome older man watering his roses. He has a beautiful garden. He smiles at her and her heart starts to pound. She wonders if he could be Morgan.

An athletic man zooms by on a bicycle and waves to the man watering his roses. Maybe the cyclist is Morgan.

Every middle-aged man she sees might be Morgan, and every house she passes might be his. She finds herself rejecting or accepting Morgan depending on the conditions of the various front yards — her preference being for wilder places with abundant flowers.

It occurs to her that she has undoubtedly seen Morgan dozens of times — in the grocery story, at the bakery, in the post office — which means he has probably seen her, although nowadays she feels mostly invisible to men.

She has Morgan's number. She told Derek she didn't want it, but he recited the seven digits anyway and she reflexively wrote them down. She has been lonely for a lover for much longer than the three years since her divorce. She and Derek stopped connecting sexually a decade before they finally parted. She knows she stayed with him out of fear of being alone, and because she didn't believe herself capable of attracting another partner.

As she passes a front yard ablaze with hundreds of roses, she imagines calling Morgan, meeting him, and falling in love with him as he falls in love with her. She smiles at how ironic it would be if love finally came to her because of Derek.

In the middle of Dorothy's description of her latest interaction with Derek, Lisa grimaces and says, "So, are you gonna call him? Morgan?"

Dorothy sighs and shrugs and feels like crying.

"He might be here right now," says Lisa, scanning the patio. "He might be that handsome hunk at the next table."

"I'm not going to call him." Dorothy closes her eyes. "What could I possibly say to him? Hi. My name is Dorothy and my verbally abusive, sexually incompetent ex-husband who treated me like dirt for eighteen years thinks you and I would be perfect for each other?"

"Why do you even *talk* to Derek?" Lisa frowns and makes a spluttering noise. "He's so devious. He's so manipulative. It's disgusting."

"We're friends," says Dorothy, shrugging again and slowly shaking her head.

"*Friends*? Gimme a break. If he was your friend he would

introduce you to the man, not give you some number to call. He's playing with you."

"Why would he do that?" Dorothy stares vacantly at her salad. "Why would he waste his time?"

"He's sick, honey. Remember your eighteen years of hell with him, and why your friends thank God every day you're not with him anymore?"

Dorothy throws away Morgan's number and ceases to think about him — whoever he might be — until one morning Derek slips a note under her front door.

> *Dear Dorothy,*
> *I had dinner at Morgan's last night. He says you haven't called him yet. He thinks you're not interested. I said you're shy. His address is 1157 3rd Street if you'd rather write to him or just walk over and say hello. He's literally around the corner from you. We could have shouted at you from his backyard and you would have heard us. He's a writer, a very good one, and he works at home. You'll really like him. He's very interested in you. What are you afraid of? I hope you won't let my involvement spoil what I truly believe is the chance of a lifetime.*
> *Love,*
> *Derek*

Dorothy sits at her altar and meditates until the bells of St. Anthony's announce noontime Mass. She opens her eyes, strikes a match, lights Derek's note on fire, and watches the words turn to ashes in her altar bowl.

Greatly relieved, she goes to her kitchen table and writes a short letter to Derek that concludes,

> *When I imagined how you would feel if you were put in my position, I understood that your motive in giving me Morgan's phone number and address was to humiliate me. Whether this was your conscious intention or not is irrelevant. Ours is not a healthy connection. I do not want to hear from you again. If you call or write, I will not answer you. Please honor my wish to terminate all contact.*
>
> *Dorothy*

BOWING

Frank, a graceful fellow of sixty-three, with sparkling blue eyes and a leonine mane of gray hair, rises from his chair to greet Kathleen with a formal politeness she both admires and mistrusts. For Frank, such courtesies are reflexive. Raised in an upper-class home in Charleston, South Carolina, he would no more stay seated at the approach of a guest, male or female, than he would allow an elder to stand on a crowded bus if he had a seat to give up to them.

Kathleen — an exuberant redhead of sixty-one — blushes as Frank takes her hand and bows, his eyes fixed on her slender fingers. Kathleen bows, too, though with obvious self-consciousness. Bowing of any kind — even among her fellow Buddhists — makes her uneasy. No matter how sincere the act, bowing reminds her of the era before the emancipation of women — and of men, too! — from superfluous social constraints and affectations.

Seated across from Frank — the sunny café bustling with vociferous diners — Kathleen smiles vivaciously and asks, "Any word?"

"None audible." Frank smiles warmly as he surveys the menu. "Which means he'll be here any minute."

"Well, I'm glad he's not here yet. I wanted some time alone with you." She reddens. "To make sure we're on the same page."

"I assure you," says Frank, gazing at her with a mixture of admiration and desire, "that whatever page you wish to be on, I will be overjoyed to be on it with you."

"I mean about the money," she half-whispers. "Did you know he currently has *three* books on the bestseller list? *No Big Deal, Beware Idiot Compassion*, and as of yesterday *Why Not Smile?* I called my friend Linda at the Expanding Awareness Forum and she said he must be getting a fortune for an *hour*, and we want him for a whole weekend."

"Oh, he doesn't care about money," says Frank, beckoning to their waiter. "Besides, he's an old friend."

Kathleen stiffens. Frank is renowned in their community for claiming to be close friends with a handful of the most famous Buddhist teachers in the world, and Kathleen is the only member of the *sangha* who believes him. No one denies Frank's profound grasp of the dharma, and everyone admires his articulate interpretations of the essential metaphors. But on those rare occasions when he mentions his personal connection to a star of contemporary Buddhism, he is instantly reduced to an object of pity and contempt in the eyes of his fellow practitioners.

Kathleen's persistent defense of Frank is invariably met with the same rebuttal. "If he's on such intimate terms with these people, why doesn't he invite one of them to address us?"

"We've only got a thousand dollars," she murmurs, succumbing to doubt for the first time in her long friendship with Frank. "It may not be enough."

"That's plenty." He nods at the approach of their waiter. "Besides, whatever you pay him, he'll just give it back to you."

"How well do you know him?" she asks, her voice freighted with worry.

Frank opens his menu and gazes up at their very tall waiter. "Yes, we'd like to start with a pot of your new Nilgiri. Blazing hot, please."

Kathleen looks at her watch. The man who is arguably the most sought after teacher in the world is a half hour late — if he was ever really coming. Until this moment, she has refused to believe what everyone else in the *sangha* has always believed, that Frank is at least a liar, at best delusional.

"Do you think I don't know him?" he asks quietly.

"You claim to know lots of people," she replies with a touch of hysteria. "But we've never met any of them."

"We?" Frank nods graciously as the waiter sets an iron teapot and two white porcelain cups on the table.

"The…our community," says Kathleen, feeling the collective scorn of the *sangha* speaking through her.

"And you actually believe that I would promise to engage this wonderful man and then stage his non-appearance to impress you?" Frank cocks his head and frowns. "Wouldn't that, in effect, put the lie to my charade?"

"Frank," she says, stunned by his precise elucidation of the case against him. "I didn't mean…"

"I had hoped, of course, that you were not of that particular group mind. And I don't believe you were until today." He fills a cup and hands it to her. "How ironic, and yet how perfect, that you should turn against me today of all days."

"I haven't turned against you." She searches his face for the slightest hint of deceit. "I haven't."

"I'm glad to hear that." He tastes his tea and arches an eyebrow. "And I'm glad we got this tea. It's exquisite."

Kathleen sips the tea, but is too upset to note the taste. She closes her eyes and finds that she has come to a major fork in the road of her life — her choice a faint path leading up a steep incline or a well-paved thoroughfare peopled with Frank's detractors. She hesitates only a moment before turning away from the crowd and climbing into the unknown.

"Ah," says Frank, rising from his chair. "Here he is now."

Now Kathleen rises, too, and opens her eyes to behold the man she has seen in a thousand pictures.

He is far more slender than she imagined he would be, and far more beautiful. His glossy black hair, cascading to his waist, is festooned with dozens of golden nasturtiums. His cotton trousers are black; his long-sleeved shirt is gray. His feet are shod in brown leather sandals, and his belongings consist of a small wicker suitcase and a walking stick — nothing more.

He pauses a few paces from their table and sets his suitcase and stick on the floor. Now he bows to Frank, bending from the waist, his hands pressed together and held over his heart. Frank bows deeply in response, and they hold their reverent poses until some message passes between them and they move in the same moment to resume their standing postures.

Now they embrace, Frank crying, "You old rascal, you."

He laughing, "My dearest friend."

GREED

Gwen makes a second attempt to read the letter from her sister, but she is too enraged to get beyond the opening sentence.

> *Dear Gwen,*
> *As you know, Dad left it to me to dispose of his*
> *possessions, and since you said you didn't want*
> *anything, I'm keeping the Marta Fuerza paintings and*
> *selling everything else.*

Gwen picks up the phone and punches her sister's number, but hangs up before the call can go through. She takes a deep breath and slowly taps Ina's number.

Ina answers after two rings. "Gwen?"

"How do you *do* that?" asks Gwen, her rage momentarily defused by Ina's clairvoyance. "With all the hundreds of people who must call you?"

"Only a few people have this number," says Ina, her voice lacking its usual resonance. "Come help me harvest snow peas?"

"I'm in a rotten mood," says Gwen, her anger getting the best of her again. "I'm furious with my sister."

"Come over." Ina's voice falls to a whisper. "I've got some furies of my own working."

Ina's garden of herbs and vegetables covers seven broad terraces ascending a gently sloping hill. A well-known horticulturist and Buddhist teacher, Ina has withdrawn from lecturing to devote herself to her husband and friends. She is forty-five, with a girlish face, enormous almond eyes, and short brown hair.

Gwen, forty-seven, is a very tall forest ranger, a pretty woman with a tendency to frown. She cut off her dark red tresses and shaved her head on the day she returned from her father's funeral, and now, a month later, her scalp is covered with fine red fuzz. Formerly a recalcitrant Episcopalian, Gwen converted to Buddhism seven years ago after hearing Ina speak.

Ina, wearing her customary long skirt and loose-fitting blouse, stands beside a hedge of pale green vines, filling a basket with snow peas. Gwen, in blue jeans and a black sweatshirt, works alongside her, picking the snow peas growing too high for Ina to reach without a ladder.

"He *promised* me one of those paintings," says Gwen, bitterly. "She was there when he promised that painting to me. She's just doing this to make me beg."

"How many paintings are there?" Ina sighs, her basket nearly full. "Of the Fuerzas?"

"Three. But there's only one I want, so of course my sister wants it, too, but only because he promised it to me. She's so vindictive. She's never forgiven me for not coming home more often. She doesn't think I deserve anything. She hates that he loved me. So now she's getting her revenge."

"Describe the painting," says Ina, setting her basket in the shade. "Let's walk down to the creek. Get wet."

"It's a still life," says Gwen, following Ina down the well-worn trail. "A white vase overflowing with yellow and white mums and blood-red roses — fallen petals on the tablecloth."

"What color is the tablecloth?" Ina takes Gwen's hand as the path descends steeply to the gurgling brook.

"Pale pink." Gwen can see every detail of the painting. "There's a coffee stain on the tablecloth in the foreground. When I was a girl I used to think it was a stain on the painting. It never occurred to me that an artist might intentionally paint a blemish on something so beautiful."

"And the background?"

"Black," says Gwen, awed by the depth of that darkness. "Pure black. But the flowers and the vase are washed in sunlight. It's all very realistic and yet it's impossible. I just love it. And it's *mine*. It's supposed to be mine."

Ina pulls off her blouse, steps out of her sandals and skirt, and wades into the stream where it pools after a drop over a jumble of gray and brown boulders — the water up to her waist. She closes her eyes and moans at the cool tug of the current.

"I know I'm being petty," says Gwen, sitting on a log to take off her running shoes. "But I can't help it. It's the *only* thing I wanted from my father. And she knows it."

"Have you asked her for the painting?" asks Ina, lowering herself into the stream — her nipples growing taut in the cold.

"No," says Gwen, stepping into the water. "Oh, my God, this feels good."

"Doesn't it?" says Ina, pressing her wet hands to her burning cheeks. "Isn't life the craziest thing?"

"What do you mean?" asks Gwen, suddenly aware of the sorrow in her teacher's voice.

"You wanting that picture with your entire being, and me..." She takes a deep breath. "...finding out a few minutes before you called that my husband isn't coming home from New Mexico."

Gwen gasps. "He's dead?"

"No." Ina submerges all but her head. "He's found another woman he prefers to me."

"He's lost his mind. How could he do this to you?"

"I was gone too much," says Ina, closing her eyes. "He was unsatisfied, and he felt overburdened with the children."

"But you came home. What more did he want?"

"I waited too long." Ina dunks her head underwater and pops back up. "No one's to blame."

"I feel like such an idiot," says Gwen, about to cry. "Whining about some stupid painting when you've just lost your husband."

"Oh, he's not lost," says Ina, smiling shrewdly. "And your painting isn't stupid. The difficulty we confront, as my teacher likes to say, is our attachment to those little buggers."

"My sister," Gwen gasps, placing her hand on her heart. "It's about my sister, not about the painting."

"Yes," says Ina — her own sorrow defined. "She misses you."

Heaven and Hell

On their way to a matinee of the San Francisco Ballet, Roger and Susan must stand for the entire journey in a crowded subway car. They are wearing heavy coats on this chilly November day, though inside the slow-moving train it is a veritable sauna — the air conditioning having failed.

Susan is twenty-six, a fetching brunette, and Roger is forty-nine, a strikingly beautiful former ballet dancer turned fashion designer. They have known each other for exactly one year, Susan and her two young children having moved from homelessness into the collective household where Roger and his lover Paul have been mainstays for more than a decade.

Paul and Roger were friendly and cordial with Susan for the first few months after she moved in, but they did not become close friends with her until they undertook their annual production of the community musical and Susan became their indefatigable assistant — Paul directing, Roger the choreographer and costume designer.

Rehearsals for the play — *Guys and Dolls* — proceeded splendidly until a week before opening night when the lead actress — with three big songs and two extravagant dance numbers — fell seriously ill. Paul was about to cancel the show when Susan shyly suggested she could play the part.

"I was a pom-pom girl in high school," she told them,

blushing at her confession. "Back in Tennessee? And I've been singing since I was a little kid. Mostly in the shower. But I can sing on key, and I know all the lines, so..."

To their great relief and astonishment, Susan was not only good in the part, she was fantastic. The play, which tradition-ally ran for two weekends, played to sold out houses for *five* weekends, and Susan became both a local star and the apple of Roger's show-business eye.

Susan was not as awed by her success as Roger and Paul were, and she returned without complaint to being a breakfast wait-ress in a nearby café and a mom afternoons and evenings.

Roger, however, was eager for Susan to pursue a show busi-ness career, for he saw her as a modern hero triumphing against all odds — with talent worthy of the professional stage.

Paul cautioned Roger about transferring his own frustrated ambition onto Susan, but Roger waved the warning aside, say-ing, "Oh, I'm just having fun. I just want her to *see* things so she can get a feel for the magic of it all."

A voice crackles over the train's public address system. "We apologize for the delay. We will be traveling at half-speed due to construction work. The air-conditioning outage is due to an electrical problem. We apologize for the crowding. Two trains ahead of us went out of service unexpectedly. Thank you for your patience. Have a nice day."

Roger, sweating profusely, shakes his head in dismay. "And they want to *encourage* the use of public transportation? Ha!

This is a farce."

Susan takes off her coat revealing her newly created dress, a svelte blue sheath designed and sewn by Roger. The train screeches to a halt and Susan is thrown against a burly man in a gray business suit. "Sorry about that," she says, righting herself. "Did I hurt you? I'm so sorry."

"Not at all." The man smiles wearily and wipes his brow with a white handkerchief. "This is insane."

"I've never been on the subway before." She grins at him. "I think it's wonderful."

"This is *not* wonderful," says Roger, running a hand through his perfectly coifed silver hair. "This is *hell*."

"At least we're moving again," says Susan, nodding hopefully as the train lurches forward. "I'm not at work. And I don't have the kids, much as I love them. And it's my birthday. I'm going to the ballet. What could be better than that?"

"We could be sitting in an air-conditioned train going fast." Roger closes his eyes. "This is a nightmare."

They detrain an hour later in downtown San Francisco, Susan following Roger through the bustling throng to an escalator blockaded with a big Out Of Order sign.

"This is too much," says Roger, starting up the stairs. "A four-story climb after sweating like pigs for an hour? This is criminal."

"Yeah, but we're here!" Susan tugs at his coattails. "I'm so excited, Roger. This is just so great."

The automatic turnstile won't let Susan exit the underground. So while Roger waits impatiently on the other side of the barrier, Susan approaches the station attendant in the big glass cubicle to find out why her ticket has been rejected. The attendant — a woman with sad brown eyes and silver fingernails — is talking on her mobile phone, oblivious to Susan.

Roger shouts, "Hurry up! We'll miss the opening piece!"

The attendant doodles on a notepad and says into her phone, "No, baby, we went there yesterday. I'm tired of Chinese. Let's do Mexican today. Chile rellenos sound *real* good to me right about now."

"Excuse me." Susan nods politely to the attendant. "I'm late for a ballet show and my ticket…"

The attendant snatches the card from Susan and sticks it into a slot on her computer console. "Not Maria's," she says, continuing her phone conversation. "Let's go to Cha Cha's. Better margaritas. Hold on." She hands the card back to Susan. "There's no credit on this. You need to add three dollars and seventy cents at the Add Credit machine."

"But I paid ten dollars in Berkeley," says Susan, her eyes filling with tears. "And I don't have any more money with me."

"Sorry," says the attendant, yawning. "Machine says that card is dead."

"Jesus!" cries Roger, waving his arms at Susan. "What the hell's going on?"

Susan shrugs helplessly. "She says my ticket doesn't have any credit. And I didn't bring any more money."

Roger storms up to the cubicle and shouts through the glass. "Now wait just a goddamn minute. We put ten dollars on that card in Berkeley. Our train was a half hour late, the air conditioning didn't work, the escalators are broken, and now…"

"You want to talk to my supervisor?" The attendant glares out at Roger. "You want to file a complaint?"

"No, ma'am," says Susan, speaking softly. "None of this is your fault. We know that. But the thing is, it's my birthday and Roger is taking me to my first ballet. I just love to dance. And he *was* a ballet dancer. And we're awful late, so…"

"Okay, go on," says the attendant, buzzing open the gate. "And teach your friend some manners."

They race along the crowded sidewalks, arriving at the theater *just* as the performance is about to begin, and despite Roger's anguished protests, they are compelled to wait in the lobby until the first piece is completed.

Roger falls onto a sofa and buries his face in his hands. "But this was the piece we wanted you to see. This is the main reason we came. This dance is *about* you, about your life."

Susan sits beside him and puts her arms around him. "Roger. It's okay, honey. There's four more dances after this one. And this is the most beautiful theater I've ever seen. Look at those stairways and those chandeliers. Isn't this amazing?"

He looks up at her, his cheeks streaked with tears. "But we wanted so much for you to see *this* piece. Paul will be crushed. We wanted this day to be perfect for you."

"It is," she says, smiling at the usher, a grim little man in a gray uniform barring their way to seats in the seventh row. "It *is* perfect. I love everything about it."

The door behind the usher opens a crack and a wizened face appears, its twinkling eyes meeting Susan's, its lips communicating something that causes the usher to beckon to Susan and Roger.

"Come in," says the usher. "There's been a slight delay. You have just enough time to get to your seats."

KILLING BUDDHA

"Can you," says Ina, an enchanting sylph of forty-nine, "elucidate your beliefs that are becoming rules?"

Matthew, sixty, a sturdy, youthful fellow, can hardly believe his ears. Nothing in his previous conversations with Ina has prepared him for such an intellectual outburst.

She taps his hand. "Now tell me the first thing that came into your mind when I asked you to do that."

"You," he says, reddening. "I saw you falling through a trap door and disappearing.

"Oh, that's wonderful," she cries, clapping her hands. "Shanghaied into nothingness."

"And I was back in school having to know the right answer." He sighs with relief. "Thank God I'm not and I don't."

"Know the right answer or writhe in shame," she intones, imitating a stentorian teacher.

Matthew and Ina are sharing the smaller of two sofas in her living room, sunlight slanting through the west-facing windows — day's end in December. She is wearing a long brown skirt and a pale blue sweater. He is in black slacks and white dress shirt, uncharacteristically fancy duds for him.

"I'm having a particular kind of difficulty, Ina." He meets her confident gaze. "Need I elaborate? Or is it obvious to you?"

"Not *too* obvious," she replies, enjoying his honesty. "But clear."

"If you were my therapist, I believe they would call this transference." He looks away from her. "But you're not my therapist."

"No?" She rises. "Tea?"

"I don't think of you as my therapist," he says, following her into the kitchen, loving the way she moves with such easy swinging grace. "Do you think of me as your client?"

"No." She fills the kettle and sets it atop the flame. "I think of you as Matthew."

"And what do you think of Matthew?" He clears his throat. "The man."

"As opposed to?" She arches an eyebrow. "The woman?"

"The person." He coughs. "You know what I mean."

She peers into her cupboard at the row of tea canisters. "I like you. Green or oolong?"

"You choose," he says, disappointed with the brevity of her reply. "I'm easy."

She smiles. "Remember what that used to mean? When a girl was easy?"

"That's how I meant it," he says, laughing. "I think."

"If only we didn't think so much of the time," she says, selecting a dark Nilgiri. "We practice and practice day after day, year after year, and only once in a great while do the engines of thought subside for a moment." She wrinkles her nose. "Tulku somebody or other said that."

Matthew sits at the table and follows her with his eyes, memorizing her face and form and movements in anticipation of never seeing her again. "What shall I do with my attraction to you? With my sense that you are attracted to me?"

"I was married and had my children," she says, blinking in surprise at her choice of words. "These years of aloneness have allowed me to deepen my practice."

"Why can't the deepening continue within a marriage?" He watches her fingers close around the handle of the kettle. "What did the Buddha say about marriage?"

"No one knows what the Buddha said about anything." She fills the teapot with boiling water. "Why do you say *marriage* instead of *relationship*?"

"Because I want to marry you," he replies, watching her face. "In a gaudy Buddhist ceremony, after which we honeymoon for a month in the wilderness."

She frowns at him. "Just the two of us? Then what?"

"Then we come back to our community and make gardens and music and meals. And love." He sighs, content with his vision of their life together. "Nice, huh?"

"To what end?" she asks, spooning the leaves into the pot.

"Happiness. Pleasure. Mystery. Death." He nods gratefully as she places the teapot on the table. "For moments like this one."

She sits opposite him, perfectly centered on her chair. "Would you marry me if you knew we would never make love?" She lifts the lid of the teapot and fills the air with a scent of India.

"Would you join me in intimate celibacy? A nun married to a monk?"

"Not yet," he whispers, reaching out to tap her hand. "Now tell me the first thing that comes into your mind."

"We're together," she says, pouring their tea. "It's an illusion we've ever been apart. Or that we know anything."

"Ina," he says, moving swiftly to her side. "I'm going to kiss you."

"Why?" she asks, assenting with her eyes.

"To murder Buddha." He draws her out of her chair. "To wallow in illusion with you. To see what happens. To see what doesn't happen."

They kiss long and lusciously, Ina pulling back for a moment to catch her breath and say, "No mind."

LOVE

Joe loves Kyle, and Kyle loves Joe. They tell each other so every day. Kyle is usually the first to say "I love you," in a whisper, tentatively, as if he's afraid the words will frighten Joe, though they always bring a smile to Joe's craggy face — a smile that changes Kyle from a sad child into a beaming boy.

Kyle is eight, Joe is seventy-two. They have known each other for two years, being members of the same Buddhist community. Kyle was homeless with his mother, Susan, and sister, Ashley, for much of his first six years, and Joe's kindness allowed Susan to move with her children from a terrifying existence on the streets to a sweeter life among friends.

Joe and Kyle do not live in the same house, but they spend time together almost every day. On Tuesday and Thursday afternoons, Joe walks Kyle from school to Chaco's café where Susan is a waitress. Joe has tea and Kyle has cocoa, and sometimes they split a piece of pie. From Chaco's, they go to Joe's house and either build things in Joe's shop or sit in the kitchen giving technical support to Agnes, one of Joe's housemates, as she cooks and bakes and sews.

On Monday, Wednesday, and Friday evenings, Joe baby-sits Kyle and Ashley while Susan goes to her tap dancing and singing lessons. On Saturdays and Sundays something invariably throws Joe and Kyle together, and when Joe goes out of town, he calls Kyle every night before bedtime so they can tell each other about their days.

One Saturday morning in April — a night of rain having cleared away the dust and smog — Joe and Kyle are turning the soil in the community garden plot where Joe grows vegetables and flowers. Joe watches Kyle grasp the stout handle of the shovel and step up onto the footholds where he rocks his sixty pounds back and forth to sink the blade into the ground. Now he dismounts and pulls back on the handle to pry the little piece of earth away from its bed and bring air and light into the soil where the new seeds will fall.

The sight of Kyle digging is so emotionally overwhelming for Joe that he cannot contain his tears.

Kyle sees Joe crying and rushes to his side. "What's wrong?" he asks, taking his great friend's hand in both of his. "What, Joe?"

"Happy," Joe manages to say as he picks the boy up and holds him on his hip. "Just happy."

Late that night, Joe taps on Agnes's bedroom door. She is sitting up in bed — glasses perched on the tip of her nose — reading the Diamond Sutra — her face youthful in the lesser light beyond the main flood of the lamp.

Joe's eyes are bleary from weeping, his hands trembling. "I...I can't stop crying."

"Come here, sweetheart." She pats the bed beside her. "Talk to me."

He sits beside her and gropes for her hand. "I can't bear the thought of Kyle dying, Agnes. It's too much for me."

"You need to cry," she says, holding him as he sobs. "This is good, Joe. This is good."

He relaxes against her, knowing she prefers his full weight to his holding himself away from her. "It would be easier," he says softly, "if he didn't love *me* so much."

"What fun would that be?" She kisses the top of his head. "Wouldn't be love if it only went one way."

Joe sits up, his sorrow blown away by sudden insight. "I need to tell him about Tommy. I thought I could *never* tell him. But it's the obstacle, isn't it?"

"Seems so," says Agnes, reaching out to him. "I miss your body on mine."

A few mornings later, Susan and Kyle sit with Joe in his sunny kitchen — Agnes gone with Ashley to feed the ducks in the park. Susan has been told in advance what Joe wants to share with Kyle, and she has given Joe her unconditional approval.

Kyle knows something is up, but he puts on a brave face and waits patiently for the adults to speak first.

"So, buddy," says Joe, swallowing his tears, "I want to tell you about something that happened to me a long time ago, something very sad about somebody you remind me of, which is why I've been crying so much lately."

"I bet I know what it is," says Kyle, afraid to look at Joe.

"What do you bet it is?" asks Joe, curious to hear what Kyle will say.

"You had a son," says Kyle, nodding. "And he ran away and you think I'll run away, too, but I never will."

"He didn't run away," says Joe, gazing in wonder at Kyle. "He died when he was five. And I've never let myself love another child until you."

Kyle, startled, looks at Joe. "Hey, and I never loved another man until you."

"What other man did you love?" asks Susan, shocked by Kyle's reply.

"My dad," says Kyle, smiling shyly. "Even if I don't remember him."

ALREADY BROKEN

They are in their kitchen — morning light making enormous shadows. Elise sits at the table, sketching with charcoal on white paper — sweet peas in a vase. Theodore stands at the sink, gazing out the window at the sheltering oaks.

"What if," he posits to her, "I no longer believe I am much of a writer?"

"I would say you were feeling insecure." She looks up from her drawing to assess the expression on his face — his brow deeply furrowed.

"But what if my belief is objective?"

She laughs. "What if my fantasies are factual?"

"Let me restate this." He sips his tea, surprised to find it isn't coffee, though he hasn't had coffee in years. "What if I *knew* I was not much of a writer?"

She shrugs. "Your knowing would disagree with mine."

"I'm going for a walk," he growls, feeling raw.

"Take some water," she says, no nonsense in her voice.

Sitting on the sand, his back against a driftwood log, he begins to meditate by focusing his attention on his out-breath.

He closes his eyes and sees his mother leering at him, her eyes bleary with rage. "You worthless piece of shit!" she screams. "You worthless piece of shit!"

"Memory," he murmurs, labeling the experience and bringing his attention back to his out-breath.

Now he feels the cool Pacific breeze caressing his face. He falls to marveling that it took him fifty years to fulfill his dream of living near the ocean. But before he can sink into regret, he labels the process — thinking — and brings his attention back to his out-breath.

Slowly, mindfully, he drinks the water his lover reminded him to bring. He watches the waves breaking on the shore — glassy walls of water shattering into foam and sound.

He opens his notebook and writes

> The vase, the cup, the body,
> the waves — already broken
> in their seeming wholeness

DYING

Rose opens her dusky brown eyes and gazes at Ina. "I'd love a cup of tea," she says huskily. "Some Pouchong, if we have any left."

Ina sets aside her knitting and rises from the rocking chair at the foot of Rose's bed. "I'll put a kettle on," she says, her long skirt rustling as she moves out of the room.

"And a biscuit or a cookie." Rose closes her eyes. "Anything."

Ina fills the silver kettle with spring water from a large earthenware crock that stands atop a table on the back porch just outside the kitchen door. Day is giving way to night. The last rays of October light slant through the forest dust — the earth and her children thirsting for rain.

Ina pauses for a moment to admire Rose's bountiful garden of vegetables and herbs, the apple orchard beyond, the mammoth redwoods in the near distance — the humid air alive with the chorusing of ten thousand crickets.

A shrill cry alerts Ina to the arrival of the resident osprey, her nest a massive basket of sticks atop the silver-gray column of a long-dead redwood, once the crown prince of the grove that was the original inspiration for Rose buying the farm.

A moment passes and the big white sea hawk drifts into view, a fat silver fish wriggling in her talons, her fledglings screeching from their nest in anticipation of a feast.

Returning with the kettle full, Ina finds Rose sitting at the kitchen table, breathing hard from the exertion of getting out of bed and walking a few steps.

"Just wanted to be up for a moment," Rose explains, taking a pale golden apple from the bowl in the center of the table. "So sweet this year."

Ina sets the kettle on the flame. "Rub your shoulders?"

"In a moment," says Rose, kissing the apple and returning it to the bowl. "I want to look at you in this light."

"We could go outside," says Ina, shaking tea leaves into the pot. "Sit on the porch swing."

"I might die out there." Rose smiles mischievously. "I feel so…insubstantial."

"Come on," says Ina, helping Rose to stand. "I'll get you settled and we'll have our tea."

"It might rain," says Rose, leaning on Ina. "Wouldn't that be lovely? We met in the rain. Remember?"

"I do," says Ina, pushing open the screen door with her foot. "You held the door for me at Café Trieste."

"We were both soaking wet," says Rose, the scene so vivid she can barely distinguish her memory of thirty years ago from their present transit to the porch. "Your face. The light in your eyes. An angel."

Ina lowers Rose onto the old swinging sofa, and tucks a pink afghan around Rose's legs. "I'll get the tea."

"Can you hear me?" asks Rose, speaking softly.

"Yes," says Ina, calling from inside. "Loud and clear."

"This dying," Rose begins, seeing the shiny tabletop in that long ago café, their bowls of coffee topped with clouds of steamed milk, "has a tangible momentum…like that fantastic acceleration toward orgasm…only the sensation extends far beyond the body and it's like I'm on a train or a moving sidewalk and the past is rushing by like scenery and I can't stop long enough to linger."

Ina sits beside Rose, holding the tea tray on her lap. "We can linger now." She pours Rose a cup of the earthy tea. "The hummingbirds have been visiting the trumpet vines and the pineapple sage all day long."

"They love those red flowers," says Rose, gazing at Ina. "Do you think this is why we met? So you would be with me when I died?"

"Yes." Ina kisses Rose's lips. "And to love each other."

"That's the only reason for anything." Rose grasps Ina's hand. "See how weak I am? Squeezing with all my might."

"Oh, look," says Ina, pointing at the garden. "The bats have come out."

"Hold me," says Rose, her vision blurring. "I'm fading."

The bats, tiny creatures the color of dusk, swoop and wheel over the garden plants, snatching gnats from the air. A flash of lightning brightens the sky beyond the redwoods — rolling thunder following.

"Now *that* seems real," says Rose, relaxing in Ina's arms. "But dying…"

A tremendous crackling accompanies a brilliant tracery of

lightning that descends into the redwoods with a deafening boom, the ground shaking from the blow, the water-laden air jarred into a sudden outpouring of rain — the parched earth hissing at the first touch of the heavenly gift.

One of the bats veers toward the house and lands with a delicate thud on the pink afghan, her oh-so-human eyes meeting Ina's before she gathers herself and wings away into the tempest.

Ina kisses Rose's cheek. "Did you see the bat, dear? Sweet little thing."

Rose does not reply — her soul departed.

About the Author

Todd Walton is a fiction writer and musician. His novels include *Inside Moves, Forgotten Impulses, Louie & Women, Night Train*, and *Ruby & Spear*. His nonfiction works include *Open Body: Creating Your Own Yoga* and *The Writer's Path: A Guidebook For Your Creative Journey*. Todd lives in Mendocino, California. His Web site is UnderTheTableBooks.com.

Photo by George Sloane

green press
INITIATIVE

Lost Coast Press is committed to preserving ancient forests and natural resources. We elected to print *Budda In A Teacup* on 50% post consumer recycled paper, processed chlorine free. As a result, for this printing, we have saved:

  11 Trees (40' tall and 6-8" diameter)
  4,549 Gallons of Wastewater
  1,829 Kilowatt Hours of Electricity
  501 Pounds of Solid Waste
  985 Pounds of Greenhouse Gases

Lost Coast Press made this paper choice because our printer, Thomson-Shore, Inc., is a member of Green Press Initiative, a nonprofit program dedicated to supporting authors, publishers, and suppliers in their efforts to reduce their use of fiber obtained from endangered forests.

For more information, visit www.greenpressinitiative.org